A Figure Rose From Behind a Mound . . .

Suddenly it was charging. Panic sent energy into my body. I groped for the gear shift and thrust it into reverse. I turned to look back. A wild, shadowed face sprung into my window. I screamed, but couldn't help staring at its eyes. I felt frozen, as if I were in a nightmare. A hand reached toward my face, clawing my throat. I thrust the gear forward and it lost its hold on the car and tumbled into the dust. Over the roar of the engine, I heard the word "curse."

DIG ME UP

SUZANNE CHANCE

AN AVON FLARE BOOK

For Stewart
With love;
And for my great-great-grandmother,
a Native American from East Texas (tribe unknown)

DIG ME UP is an original publication of Avon Books. This work has never before appeared in book form. This work is a novel. Any similarity to actual persons or events is purely coincidental.

AVON BOOKS
A division of
The Hearst Corporation
1350 Avenue of the Americas
New York, New York 10019

property of Justin Holland 4-DO

Please return!

One

The car fish-tailed out of control as I swung onto the narrow gravel road. The headlights flashed back and forth across the dark pine forest. This was the road just after the billboard, but nothing looked familiar. This was the right way, wasn't it? Uneasiness stirred inside me. My hands tightly clutched the steering wheel.

Mother would probably yell at me again, but she had to know. She would want me to sound sure of myself. She'd really light into me if I didn't sound certain.

"Mother, I've turned on the road to Frankie's house." She had nodded off again because of the migraine pills. "It's got to be this one," I mumbled to myself.

The East Texas woods closed in on each side. It was like driving into a tunnel with only a starry strip of night overhead. Something about the road felt wrong, but I just couldn't turn around. Not yet. Mother'd jump all over me for getting on the wrong road at all. There didn't seem to be enough air in the car, so I rolled down the window.

Mother sat up stiffly, blinking as if she couldn't focus. "I don't remember this. How did you get on this road, Callie? Where are the directions?" She fished around the front seats and into the back.

Maybe she wouldn't be upset. "I can't find the think they're on the kitchen table."

She stopped her search and dropped her arms. "Here I give you a little responsibility, and you can't even remember to do the simplest thing. If you go on a trip, you have to have directions. I told you yesterday to make sure you had them since you were driving."

"You were shouting a lot of things yesterday. How am I supposed to remember them all?" My lip hurt where I bit it to keep from crying.

Her body stiffened. "I don't shout. And you have a lot to remember if you're going to be a good house guest this summer. It's not going to be like home, you know. I won't be there to remember for you."

What little confidence I had crumbled.

We almost passed the opening on our left before we noticed it. "This might be the back way into her subdivision," Mother said.

The rutted dirt lane twisted through the woods and opened all at once onto a large clearing. When I pulled up beside an abandoned car, I put the car into neutral.

The golden moon, so large and bright, rose above the low hill in the center of the field. I sucked in my breath. The moonlight and long shadows made striped patterns on the meadow. Even Mother, who never seemed to have time for watching a moon rise, stared at the beautiful sight.

A figure rose from behind the mound, turned, and spread its arms as if in worship to the moon. I leaned forward. What could it be? A rhythmic chant floated across the night. The shadow took slow steps like he was doing a primitive dance. The sounds didn't seem like words, but his voice was sometimes angry, sometimes pleading.

A mosquito buzzed my left ear, then pierced my arm. I looked down to slap it. When I looked up, the figure was no longer on the mound.

I saw him charging toward us. Panic sent a large shot of energy into my body. My heart banged against my

2

chest. "We'd better get out of here!" Mother's head nodded, but she had slumped against the window with her eyes shut.

I groped for the gear shift. My hand touched the gear shift ball, and I thrust it into reverse. I revved the engine, but the gear didn't catch at once.

The car rolled backward. Suddenly, out of nowhere a wild, shadowed face sprung into my window, growling. I couldn't help staring at his eyes. Something, maybe paint, streaked his cheeks. I felt frozen, as if I were in a nightmare and couldn't move.

He reached his hand toward my face, and brought me to my senses. I pushed down hard on the accelerator. The car lurched back in a wide circle so that we pointed toward the dirt road, but the wild man hung onto the door. His hand clawed near my throat. I flung my elbow in his face. As he leaned to avoid it, I jammed the car into first. Whoever—whatever—it was lost his hold and tumbled into our dust.

In the rearview mirror, the phantom lifted his arms, this time holding them stiffly toward us. Again strange chanting drifted across the night. Despite the drone of the engine, I thought I could make out the word "curse."

My insides shuddered as Mother told the story to Frankie Stevens. The tale didn't sound anything like what had happened. The word "curse" echoed in my head over and over again. Now that we were in a brightly lit house, the details of the event were slipping away.

"Linda, you mean you and Callie were attacked?" Frankie put one of my suitcases down on a twin bed in her spare bedroom. She turned to Mother with concern.

"Oh, I was asleep and Callie took the wrong road. Some man must have gotten angry at us for trespassing, that's all. Callie's imagination has always been wild, especially when she is scared." I had embarrassed her again.

3

Maybe I had imagined some of it. My mind sometimes created daydreams that frightened me. Maybe Mother was right. My fear faded into shame that I had caused such a stir.

Mother enthusiastically described her plans for the summer. My old sadness returned. Did she want me out of her life? For the last six months, she had had no time for anything but work, work, work. Who had time for a daughter?

Mother looked over to me with doubt on her face. "Frankie, I hope you know what you're getting yourself into. Are you sure you want her for the whole summer?"

Frankie turned to me and smiled. "We'd be delighted to have you stay for as long as you like." This English professor was tall and thin like me and wearing a t-shirt and shorts. Except for a few smile lines around her eyes, she looked like a student.

"Thank you," I mumbled. More attention embarrassed me, but I was glad she wanted me here. Frankie was like an aunt to me.

They left me so that they could catch up on the latest before Mother went back to Houston in the morning. When I opened my suitcase, my journal flopped out on the bed.

The ink-filled pages fluttered over to my poem, "Rage." To outsiders, it said, we had always been the perfect mother-daughter pair. She pressured me to join all sorts of things, whether I wanted to or not. She was always doing something with the PTA, youth groups, or scouts. But it was all image.

Image. That frightening face. He cursed me.

In the other part of the house, I heard a door slam and a man's voice say hello. As I came into the den, a tall, middle-aged man was shaking Mother's hand and balancing a sack of groceries with the other arm. " . . . just sorry you won't be staying with us for a

4

while, Linda," Frankie's new husband said.

"Thank you, Walter, but I must get back to Houston early in the morning. I have a full day at the office tomorrow." Mother maintained her professional smile.

Dr. Walter Broussard's face grew serious. "We know things have been hectic lately. If there's anything we can do . . ."

"You are already doing more than you should in keeping Callie." To my surprise, Mother reached over and hugged me briefly.

Dr. Broussard turned toward me. "There you are!" He extended his big hand.

"How do you do," I responded.

"I do just fine, young lady, just fine. My, but you've become a woman since the wedding, hasn't she Frankie?" Frankie smiled. "We'll have a great time this summer. And Linda, I promise to keep an eye on all the college boys that will line up at our door to see Callie." His wink was warm and friendly.

Frankie nodded toward the sack in his arms. "Hon, do you want to put the drinks down?"

"I'll put them in the kitchen. Clyde had some cold champagne and I thought we might drink a toast to old friends." He left for some wine glasses.

Frankie looked amused as she watched him go.

"Who is Clyde?" Mother asked.

Frankie laughed. "Oh, Linda, you just wouldn't believe this husband of mine. My Dean of Social Sciences has a good buddy who runs a liquor store across the county line. We're dry here in Weches, you know."

Mother seemed to have trouble putting on her smile. A manager of a liquor store was way below her social level. "Oh, how quaint. How did they meet?"

"Well, Walt's a member of the East Texas Historical Commission and is always interested in gathering bits of local folklore. Any time he runs across a native to these parts, he asks about stories their grandmother used to tell, that sort of thing. One day when Walter went to pick up some beer, Clyde and he struck up a conversation about the way things used to be. One story led to another, and before I knew it, these trips were taking a couple of hours."

Dr. Broussard returned with a tray carrying four champagne-filled glasses. "Here we are. Linda?" He moved from Mother to me. "And we're going to let our new house guest have some, aren't we?"

Mother nodded, but held up her thumb and forefinger to let him know I couldn't have much. We toasted the summer after everyone had a glass. The champagne was cold and a little sour, and the bubbles tickled my nose.

"So what stories did your friend tell you tonight," Mother said in her making-conversation tone of voice.

"Oh, he had heard a tale of a Caddo warrior, killed by a white man hundreds of years ago, who still haunts these parts. The tale is that this spirit attacks people in remote areas. This story is common in almost every culture. Kids call it a 'bogeyman story.' I think they're made up by mothers who are trying to keep their kids in line. Did I say something wrong?" He stopped when he saw my open mouth.

Had a dead warrior cursed me? My mind whirled.

"Walt, Linda and Callie were attacked by a strange man when they became lost on their way here," Frankie explained, placing her hand on his arm.

"Oh, I'm terribly sorry. Neither of you is hurt, I hope? What happened?"

Mother shook her perfectly combed blond hair. "It wasn't that serious," she said, and repeated her watered-down version.

Dr. Broussard shook his head. "I don't understand it. Might have been one of the backwoods hermits. They can be vicious to intruders. But it sounds more like a fraternity prank. Registration for the summer term begins tomorrow so most of the students are back. I'll

6

ask around to see if the Greeks are up to something."

When my champagne was drained, their conversation had drifted from the college to politics. I excused myself, mumbling something about seeing the backyard, and stepped out to their back porch.

The moon, through a large sweet gum tree with its star-shaped leaves, cast a shadow on the ground. Down in the valley, I could just see the lights of Weches. It was a pretty town snuggled in the East Texas hills. The heat of the day had eased with a cool breeze. I flopped onto a padded chair and stared at the sky. One star twinkled brightly next to the big moon despite the strength of the moonlight.

When I realized the voices had died down inside, I glanced at my watch. More than an hour and a half had drifted by. The back door opened and Frankie's head stuck out.

"Just wanted to make sure you hadn't fallen asleep from the champagne," she said.

"No, I'm enjoying the night. The moon is beautiful."

She looked up. "It is a lovely evening, isn't it? Your mom has gone to bed and Walt and I are ready to turn in. Lock the door when you come in, ok?"

I smiled, pleased that she wasn't pressuring me to go to bed. "Sure. Good night, Frankie. And thanks."

"No problem. See you in the morning."

My head leaned back and I continued to watch the night sky. I must have dozed off, because I awoke with a start. My senses sharpened. An odd sound came from the side of the house. Was it a neighbor's television?

It sounded like the chanting of the man who had attacked me. My chest tightened with fear. I jumped off the chair and ran to the door. Was the chanting growing louder?

The handle was stuck. Frankie couldn't have locked the door. I jiggled the handle frantically, twisting my head to see if anyone was coming.

7

A twig snapped. I turned the knob slowly while pulling it toward me. The latch opened. My shoulder knocked the door wide. I stumbled into the living room and slammed it shut, locking it and putting the chain on for extra safety. In the dark room, I leaned against the door and panted.

"This is silly, Callie," I whispered. "You had a scare earlier, and now you're dreaming up ghosts. You need to go to bed."

As my eyes adjusted to the dark, I picked my way past the sofa and chairs to the hall. Before I left the room, I whirled quickly toward the window. Did a shadow move across the window or was the moonlight making strange patterns on the drapes?

I hurried to my room, eager to huddle down into the sheets, but it was a long time before I quit jumping at night noises and fell asleep.

TWO

When I woke up the next morning, my nightmares faded away, but they left me feeling uneasy. The sound of wicked laughing had haunted my dreams.

I stretched in the early morning light filling Frankie's guest bedroom. Mother's bed was neatly made with a white envelope laying in the center. She and her suitcase were gone. A hug from her would have been nice.

Inside the envelope were several twenty dollar bills. On a sheet of paper she had written, "Dear Callie, I hope you have a good summer. Try to make good decisions. I'll call and write you from time to time. If you need more money, let me know. Be the perfect guest. Give Frankie and Walter plenty of time by themselves. Love, Mother."

The crumpled note hit the trash can. She didn't understand that I wanted her, not the money. With effort, I pushed the blues away and dressed.

Frankie sat in the old-fashioned olive green kitchen drinking coffee and sorting through a mess of papers on the breakfast table. A strand of dark hair had fallen from her ponytail. "Morning, Callie. There's still some coffee left in the pot. How'd you sleep?"

I poured myself a cup. "So-so, I guess. Where is everybody?"

"Walt's already at Summer Registration. I'm not due there for another hour. Your mom left as Walt was getting up. So you didn't sleep so well?"

I didn't look at her as I shook my head because I knew I might cry. Her voice softened. "That incident last night must have frightened you. You haven't had a chance to talk about it. Did you have bad dreams?"

I nodded, feeling like I should be more grown up about it. But her concern comforted me. I sat across from her and sipped the hot coffee.

"You know, I never did hear your version of things. I gathered that your mom didn't see everything. Want to tell me about it?"

Immediately, my story and my fears poured out. I told her everything, including that I felt responsible for picking the wrong road, and how I caused the whole thing. Then I mumbled that I probably imagined most of it, anyway.

She put her coffee cup down and looked at me sternly. "Callie, you're being too hard on yourself. I believe you. You tell the story with such detail, you couldn't possibly have made it up. Like you said, your mom slept through most of it, so she didn't see everything."

She shook her head to herself, glanced up at the ceiling and sighed. "You know, it sounds to me as if you haven't learned to trust yourself. Try this: If the whole thing had happened to me, and I was telling you, what would you say to me?"

My eyebrows raised in surprise as I tried to picture her telling the story. "Well, I guess I'd say you were brave to have fought the guy off. And you saved both you and Mother." I stopped. "Oh." I said.

She smiled. "Right. You were the brave one. You are the hero for fighting the guy off."

I shook my head. "I guess it's true, but somehow, I have a hard time believing it. I just don't see myself as a hero."

10

"I can see we have at least one project for the summer."

"What's that?"

Frankie smiled. "Working on your self-esteem. And speaking of the summer, I know that it's going to be awkward for you at first, but I want you to be comfortable with us. For weeks, I've looked forward to you coming."

"Why?"

She reached across the table and patted my hand. "Because I like you, Callie. I always have. You're a kind, sensitive, wonderful person. I know it must difficult to be compared to your mother. It'll be fun having you around this summer. I hope you enjoy it."

It was hard believing all those nice things, but it made me feel better. "I'm sure I will," I said. Maybe she and I could spend time together.

She nodded as if she had accomplished something. "Good. Now let's see. We have some eggs and cereal, and there's a coffee cake in the fridge. What can I get you?"

"Cereal's fine. And I can get it."

As I ate she explained that she and Dr. Broussard would be busy with Registration until evening. "Why don't you spend the day getting familiar with the campus? You'll be deciding on a college soon, so you might as well take the opportunity to look over ours."

I nodded as I chewed. Exploring the campus sounded fun.

"This evening, Walt and I have been invited to a faculty picnic. I thought you might like to join us. There'll be people there your age." She wiggled her eyebrows. "Remind me to point out Bart Petersen. He's certainly worth taking a peek at, and happens to be a nice guy on top of it. Of course, it's up to you whether you want to go with us or not."

It struck me that I still hadn't decided what I was going

11

to do with myself all summer. Job? School? Loafing? "Sure. That sounds fine."

She stood to go. She picked a few pieces of lint off her green leaf-print blouse and soft brown skirt. She gathered her papers and placed them in a brown folder. "I've got to drop these off at the department before I hit Registration. Here's a map of the campus. You can use my bike in the garage. The key and lock are around the handlebars. See you tonight." She opened the door to the garage and left.

Frankie's bike cruised smoothly toward the campus. The tree-lined streets of the quiet neighborhood wound around and eventually flowed into the University. As I pedaled along sidewalks and bike paths, I felt a little out of place, but no one seemed to notice that I was different.

After weaving through brown brick buildings, tall pines and sweet gum trees, I found the Student Union and went inside. Down the wide corridors past the cafeteria, a post office and book store, I came to a large lobby filled with students. I browsed through some of the fliers on a table.

A student burst through the double doors and ran to the guys next to me. "Hey, you ought to come see the protest that's going on. It's like something out of the sixties!"

I leaned slightly closer to listen to him.

"What protest?"

"Who's protesting where?"

"They're Caddo Indians in full costume carrying picket signs in front of Social Sciences. They're protesting some sort of dig that Archaeology is going to do this summer. Someone's gone for the University Police. You've got to come see!"

A small fear shivered up my spine when he mentioned a fully costumed Caddo Indian. I pictured the distorted face in my car window. A Caddo warrior, Dr. Broussard had said. Had it been an Indian who had tried to kill me? My heart beat faster, but I followed the group out the door and into a large courtyard.

On the steps of the nearest building were six or seven Native Americans walking a picket line and all around them a large crowd had formed. I snaked through the students to get closer. "Maybe the man last night is one of these people," I thought, but didn't know what I'd do if he was. What would I tell the police? *Officer, this man ran after me and made an ugly face in my window after I trespassed on his land?* The police would never believe me, not with a story like that. I couldn't help but feel ridiculous.

I planted myself a few rows back and watched the picketers' faces as they circled around. All were college age, and two were women. Some were nervous and looked anxiously at the crowd; others were proud and defiant. None had the face of my attacker. But how I could be sure, since the man's face had been in shadows?

Two signs they carried read: "When will the White Man's rape stop?" and "Is nothing sacred?" A tall young man with a serious expression but wearing street clothes handed his picket to another and stepped back. His face seemed sad, so I edged closer to him. Now I felt certain that the leader wasn't my attacker, though I couldn't say why.

He spoke to the crowd. "This is what we hoped would happen. People are thinking and talking about us. We will be in the school and local newspapers, and then the issue will be before the public. It is against the law to disturb a white man's grave without family permission and a court order. Why should it be any different for the graves of Caddoes who lived several hundred years ago?"

A student next to me stepped forward. "But surely they are only trying to study ancient cultures and learn from them so that all will benefit." She sounded as if she were quoting a textbook.

He turned a harsh eye on her. His strong cheekbones were made more prominent by the tension in his face. "And how would you feel if someone wanted to dig up the bones of your grandparents and great-grandparents to put them on display in a museum so that all might learn from them?" She opened and closed her mouth, as if trying to think of a reply.

I turned away when I heard the doors of the building behind me open. Out came Dr. Broussard, followed by several campus police. They glanced around and spotted the Indian next to me.

Dr. Broussard approached him. "Look, I was willing to let this go on so long as it didn't make too much of a commotion. I'm afraid the police will have to escort you off campus. I hope you'll cooperate."

The young man gave half a shrug and motioned to the others to pack their things.

"Is that it?" one guy in the crowd asked. "Is that all you're going to do for something which you supposedly believe so strongly in?"

I couldn't believe the guy had the gall to say it. But the leader's sadness and anger seemed to touch something deep within me, also. It was as if I wanted to have the courage to stand up for what I believed in, too.

He turned sharply. "What's it to you," he growled, then turned away again. He lowered his voice. "We'll be back. We're not through here." He walked away with the police.

His last words worried me. I wondered if one of the leader's friends had tried to grab my throat.

On the way over to the faculty picnic that evening, Dr. Broussard and I talked about the protest. "I have mixed feelings about it," Dr. Broussard confessed. "I can sympathize with the young Caddoes' argument that the white

14

people are again disturbing their culture. I've got a tiny bit of Caddo blood in me like a lot of people around here. But on the other hand, Native Americans have benefited from a greater understanding of their culture. Archaeologists and anthropologists can take some credit for that." When Dr. Broussard put it like that, it made me a little angry at the Caddoes.

We joined the picnic at one of the local parks. I followed Dr. Broussard and Frankie, being polite as they introduced me.

Soon, Frankie turned to me. "This isn't much fun for you, is it?" I didn't say anything, but she nodded.

"I know. I'll introduce you to the Petersens. They're not some of Walt's favorite people, but I think you'll like them. They have two kids about your age. Remember, I told you about young Bart. And Jon is in charge of the Caddo mound excavation this summer. He'd be happy to answer your questions about it."

Frankie found Dr. Jon Petersen standing in line underneath a huge oak tree waiting for his turn at the beer keg. "Jon! I'd like you to meet Calliope Davis, Callie to her friends. Walt and I are privileged to have her stay with us for the summer. She was on campus today and saw the protest. I thought you might be able to answer some of her questions."

He stuck out his brown, callused hand. "How do you do, Calliope Davis, Callie for short. Did you know that Calliope was the chief of the Muses? You've a fine heritage in that name. Sure, I'd be happy to answer your questions."

I shook his hand. This lean, muscular man with graying blond hair was handsome. I wondered if his son Bart was as good looking. "Oh, I didn't really have any questions. It's just that I heard one of the Caddoes at the protest today and it started me thinking about archaeology."

He filled his cup with beer and motioned me toward a picnic table under a large pecan tree. "That's good. I wish

15

more people would think about archaeology. What's on your mind?"

I sat down, picturing the handsome Caddo's sad face. I told Dr. Petersen how the guy felt about the excavation. "It started me thinking about all the stuff that has been taken from the Egyptian tombs and from places all over the world. The people who put those treasures there did it because of their religion. Who are we to violate their beliefs and raid the tombs and put the stuff in museums?"

He looked at me curiously for a moment. "That's a very intelligent question. How old are you?"

"Seventeen."

"I'm impressed. Well, I can't claim to have all the answers. While I was studying archaeology in school, I asked myself the same question. When the science began, explorers traveled to faraway lands on trips that took years. The explorers brought back artifacts for profit, of course, but also to be able to study them. People then, as they are now, were curious about other cultures.

"But as scientists decided to study ancient cultures more carefully, they found that small pottery fragments were often more valuable than the flashy stuff like gold or jewels. These shards told them how old the site and its contents were. The more ancient it was, the more we learned. But even these high-minded scientists had a conqueror's attitude toward the pieces they found. As we learned more, a black market arose for rich people wanting a piece of history in their own homes. It thrives today. Did you know that in many of the sites around the world, art thieves have been there first and have left only a small fraction of what was originally buried intact? Governments work with scientists to guard discoveries from the grave robbers."

His answer left me unsatisfied. "But that's a weak excuse. 'Scientists do it to beat the grave robbers to the punch.' It's still a violation of people's beliefs."

16

He arched his eyebrows. "I can't deny you have a point there. The fact remains, though, that if a site is known, or even rumored about, someone will steal the artifacts. So it's a choice between a few people who stupidly destroy a great deal of the site for a quick profit, or scientists who carefully preserve and record all that is there for the benefit of everyone. Most governments can't afford to protect all the ancient sites. I haven't heard the Caddoes offer to post some of their people to guard those mounds. And don't forget that the more the public knows about these cultures, the greater respect they give them. The Caddoes benefit from that. We learn more about their ways, and it fosters a greater understanding between everybody."

It still seemed like an excuse to rob graves. "And you enjoy what you do?"

He smiled. "Of course I do! It's an incredible feeling to uncover an object, after weeks of hot work, which is several hundred, maybe even several thousand years old. To hold something like that in your hand and realize that someone took the time to make it, that she had a family, lived and then died—well, it's indescribable." He looked at the ground as if remembering such an experience.

Even though I still felt it was wrong in a way, to dig in ancient mounds also sounded fascinating, and like it did some good.

"You know, all this isn't even the most frequent reason why sites are excavated."

"It's not?"

He shook his sandy hair. "Nope. Most archaeologists are called in when a bulldozer on a construction crew uncovers something that even ordinary people know is valuable. If the boss is sympathetic, then we get notified. Otherwise, it's plowed under or stolen by workers. But even if we receive notice, we often have only a week or so to save what we can. One week, when most sites would take a summer, or possibly even several years to excavate properly. That's the case with the Caddo site."

I was surprised. "But how can that be? Surely the Caddoes wouldn't protest if they knew that you would be saving what you could from a bulldozer. They might even want to help."

He leaned his back against the table, stuck his legs out and examined the blue, cloud-filled sky. "I wouldn't be surprised if they didn't know about it. Not many folks around here realize that the highway will be going through that way. Only a handful know that that's the reason the project was approved for this summer. Funds are tight, you know. Besides, even if those young people did realize that this was a salvage job, they would still protest the white man's 'progress.' I'd join them on that one. It takes a lot of money to protect a site. The politicians in Austin want to be able to turn these places into parks. They'd want to know about possible fee revenues before they'll allocate funds for anything these days. So the way I see it, it's either save what we can as quickly as possible, or let the bulldozers in."

I followed his eyes to the large white cloud overhead. "I can't believe that it comes down to a matter of money when something so important is at stake."

He turned toward me. "You know, you could do something about it."

"What, you taking up a collection, or something?"

He threw his head back and laughed. "No, but that's pretty good. You don't mind if I tell that in the department do you? No, I thought maybe you might enjoy working in the excavation—using a shovel, trowel and sifter to see what's underground. It's hard, hot, and sometimes boring work, but I think you'd find it quite a learning experience. Since you seem interested in the Caddoes, it would be a chance of a lifetime to see what they were really like."

I felt honored that he would ask me. "Don't you have professionals go in there? How are you going to get special permission for me?" And why, I wondered. I might mess it up, like taking the wrong road.

"That's what most people think. Most excavations are done by students or volunteers who are overseen by an archaeologist and maybe some assistants. We can always use a helping hand from someone genuinely interested. Field Archaeology 201 will be tackling the Caddo site this semester. I thought you might want to take the class."

"I haven't even graduated from high school. How can I take a course for college sophomores?"

"Exceptions can be made for students who will be high school seniors the following year. I can't guarantee that you'd receive college credit, but if you want the experience, I can probably get you in. And after all," he smiled, "you could talk to the Dean yourself."

This time I laughed and let him talk me into it. "And I imagine Frankie could butter him up if I couldn't. Sure, I'd love to take your course. I don't know that I've decided what to think about archaeology in general, but I'd like to help save what I can before the bulldozers come."

I felt excited and privileged to be asked to join the team. Even with some doubts, saving the site seemed like the right thing to do. Something inside me stirred, a thrill I hadn't felt in a long time. I decided to learn all I could about Native Americans this summer. Maybe then I could understand why that guy attacked me.

Some motion caught my eye at the trunk of the oak we were sitting under. "Hi, Daddy," a girl about my age said.

She was a petite blond with a perfect figure. Stacked, the guys would say. Long yellow curls hung about her round face, which would have been pretty had she not been looking at me with a mocking smile. I hated her at once.

"Can I join your course, too, Daddy?" She looked

straight at me with wicked blue eyes, smiling as if she had scored a point.

I didn't know what her story was, but this girl apparently had it in for me. I had a feeling she would try to make my summer miserable.

Three

I listened to five minutes of pleading from Dr. Petersen's eighteen-year-old daughter, Erica. Finally, Dr. Petersen raised his hands. "Enough, Erica. I can't imagine why you've become so interested in science all of a sudden, but far be it from me to discourage you. Fine. I'll make an exception for you, too."

"Oh, thank you, Daddy. You won't regret it." She kissed him on the cheek and the matter was settled. He left us alone so that we could get to know each other. I would rather have gotten to know a rattlesnake.

"So," she said with a smirk and a gaze that would melt lead, "a little high school girl has charmed my Daddy into letting her work with him. Isn't that cute? And I'll bet you're willing to help on any of those after-hours chores in the lab, aren't you?" Her smile vanished and her eyes narrowed. "I'll be watching you." She spun away before I could reply.

My mouth opened. She was jealous of me. My instincts shouted that I should grab her and shake some sense into her. I forced myself to walk calmly to a table and pick up a soft drink.

Why did she think I was flirting with her father? How ridiculous. I never flirted with him. She must be crazy. I couldn't have done something wrong again, could I?

Erica must have imagined it. I took a deep breath and forced the whole incident out of my mind.

I strolled around the park for a few moments, tiptoeing through the zebra-like bands of light and shadow across the path. The evening sun bathed the foliage in a warm peacefulness that washed away all my worries.

As I walked beyond the hedge, I saw someone crouched behind a bush near Dr. Petersen and eavesdropping on his conversation with two older students.

It wasn't really any of my business, but it seemed so sneaky, so underhanded. Since Dr. Petersen had been so kind to me, I felt protective of him and angry. I just couldn't let the guy get away with it.

I looped around so as to come on him from behind. He was a young man, I could tell, and was dark skinned. A cap hid his hair from view.

My mind flashed back to the Caddoes at the protest, and their leader's words echoed in my mind: "We'll be back. We're not through here."

I crept along the curving hedge trying to move as silently as possible. Before I even drew close, he twisted toward me, placed a finger to his lips, and turned back to continue listening.

I was appalled. How could he think that I would help him eavesdrop on Dr. Petersen? And yet, the guy seemed harmless, so I moved closer without saying anything. I picked up the conversation.

"So have you received any more threats since then?" the young woman asked.

"No." Dr. Petersen replied. "But I'd be surprised if this were the last of them. I expect things to become a lot more active this week as the excavation begins."

"Yeah, and there's not a damn thing we can do about it," the guy said. "But then the Weches Police Department probably wouldn't take it seriously anyway."

"We're just going to have to be careful and keep a watchful eye around the lab and the site," Dr. Petersen said. "Although I expect to hear from them again, I think they are only trying to frighten us off. I doubt if anyone would harm anything."

"But you don't know that to be so. Like you said, we'll have to be careful," the young woman said. Dr. Petersen urged them toward the rest of the faculty and their conversation became too faint to hear.

The fear aroused last night in the car returned. "First the protest and now these threats," I muttered. "I wonder if they're related."

"That's what I want to know," my fellow eavesdropper said, startling me.

My anger boiled to the surface again. "Who are you and why are you sneaking about listening to Dr. Petersen's conversations?"

He was amused. "And you aren't doing the same?"

"No. I saw what you were doing from across the park and came to stop you."

He took off his cap and ran his fingers through his blond, obviously not Caddo, hair. "So why didn't you?"

I didn't know what to say. I didn't know why I didn't stop him, which made me angrier. "Just answer my questions."

He looked at me with piercing blue eyes. Even before he spoke, I knew part of the answer. "If it's any business of yours, Dr. Petersen is my dad, and I'm worried about him."

"Oh." It was all I could think of to say. Once again, I had blown it.

He arched his blond eyebrows and studied me closely. "So how do you know him? You look too young to be a student at Weches State."

I blushed. "I am. I'm staying the summer with Dr. Frankie Stevens and Dr. Walter Broussard." When I mentioned Dr. Broussard's name, his eyes narrowed and

23

he frowned. "Frankie introduced me to your dad, and he suggested I take his field course. He's going to arrange special permission."

He picked at the grass. "So you'll be in his class, huh?"

"Yeah, I think so. But why is somebody threatening your dad?"

He shrugged. "I don't know. He doesn't talk about it. Mom doesn't even know. I found one of the notes, and he got mad at me and told me to forget it and not to tell anyone. From what I can figure, somebody wants to stop the dig. Dad's afraid that if others know he's being threatened, the Dean will cancel the course." His head popped up with challenge in his eyes. "I've said too much. You better not tell Dr. Broussard, or I'll—"

"Hey, wait. I'm not going to tell anybody anything." Against my better judgment, I liked Dr. Petersen's son. And he was as handsome as Frankie had said. "Frankie told me that your dad and Dr. Broussard are not exactly best friends. But just because I'm staying with him doesn't mean that I'm going to tell him everything I hear. I hardly know him myself."

He still seemed suspicious. I smiled at him. "Why don't we start this all over again. Hi. My name's Callie. What's yours?"

He gave me half a smile. "Bart."

"Hi, Bart. Since I'm going to be in your father's class this summer, why don't I keep an eye out for anything suspicious? If I think he's received another threat, I'll let you know, but no one else. You can do the same for me. Deal?"

"Why are you doing this?"

I traced a branch with my finger. "Oh, I don't know. Since I arrived in Weches last night, there have been a lot of strange things happening, some of them to me. They all have to do with Native Americans. Besides, I'm going to be in the class anyway. And you seem nice—a lot

24

nicer than your sister." As soon as I said it, I just knew he'd hate me.

He raised his blond eyebrows. "So you've met Erica, have you? We're completely different, thank goodness. How'd you meet her?"

With relief, I told him about it on the way back to the picnic. As we walked, he asked about the strange events I had mentioned. So I told him about the attack in the car, what Dr. Broussard had said about the dead warrior who attacked people in the backwoods, and the protest on campus today. He listened closely, asking about details now and then, but obviously believing everything I said.

He ran his fingers through his blond hair. "Since you seem to know so much, I think we should tell each other if we find out anything more. I'm worried about my dad."

"I think that's a good idea." We exchanged phone numbers and said good-bye. I watched him walk across the park. We hadn't talked long, but I knew Bart was the sort of guy I could trust.

We arrived back at the house after dark. Frankie decided to take a shower. Dr. Broussard suggested we sit in the backyard and drink iced tea. He lit the citronella candles in their small tin buckets to keep away mosquitoes. We relaxed in the comfortable lounge chairs, enjoying the break from the day's heat.

"Dr. Broussard."

"Yes?"

"You said you'd check around to see if the fraternities were pulling any pranks . . ."

He snapped his fingers. "Oh, Callie, I'm sorry. What with Registration and the protest, I didn't remember to call the people I meant to. I did speak with some of the Greeks, though. They hadn't heard of anyone pulling a prank like that. I'm sorry. I know it must have frightened you."

I sat forward. "No, please don't be sorry. Thanks for asking. The students would probably know more of that sort of thing anyway."

He reached across and patted my arm. His voice softened. "You know, I wouldn't worry about that sort of thing. I still think that person was just trying to scare you away. I don't think you have to worry about it happening again." Across the candlelit patio, he gave me a little smile.

Now that I thought about it, he had to be right. After all, nobody could have known I'd be driving down that road. "I guess you're right. Thanks."

He leaned his graying head back on the chair, making his slight potbelly more prominent. "So, temporary daughter, tell me about yourself. You want to take that course from Petersen this summer. How are your grades?"

I grinned at his fatherly concern. "B's mostly, but some A's and C's."

"Good. Shouldn't have any problem with the paperwork then. What're your most and least favorite subjects?"

"I like English and history, but I hate math."

He chuckled. "That sounds normal. Most of the professors in Social Sciences said the same thing at your age. So, do you have a boyfriend," he asked, but then stopped. "Look at me. I'm acting like the chief prosecutor."

I laughed at his embarrassment. "That's ok. I like talking to you." My smile fell. "No. I haven't had time for a boyfriend this year. With the divorce and all I guess I've had other things on my mind." A bitter memory returned: My tall, dark-haired dad had his arm around a short, blond woman. And then I knew why Erica made me angry. She reminded me of Dad's new girlfriend.

I turned back to Dr. Broussard. He held a hurt, angry expression as he gazed across the dark yard, and I wondered if I had made him mad. "Did I say something wrong?"

26

He shook his head. "No, sorry. I just have memories of relationships and bitter endings."

"Were you . . . divorced?"

"No, no. It didn't end that way. I couldn't divorce Melanie."

His face relaxed. "I'm terribly sorry, Callie. I didn't mean to go on like that. You think you're completely over something, then it pops up again unexpectedly." He let his head fall back and rolled it from shoulder to shoulder as if to relieve tense muscles.

"It's ok," I said again. I had always felt uncomfortable when adults got upset, so I changed the subject. "Tell me about the Caddoes. Maybe you can give me a jump on all those college students tomorrow."

He gazed into the star-thick sky. "The Caddoes? That's a long story. And folklore is my favorite topic." I sipped some tea and studied his candlelit profile.

"I think Dr. Petersen will give you a good history of them and some idea of their daily life. I'm more interested in the essence of the people, how they viewed life, their myths and religion. It's these things that make one culture different from another." He seemed excited about the subject.

"Of course, everyone must eat, sleep in shelter and wear clothes. How people do this varies across the seas and across time. But climate and location determine the differences for the most part."

He shifted in his chair, then turned to me. "Well, I could go on and on. But the important thing to me is the way people look at their daily life, their history and the natural world. That's what makes a culture unique. Their worldview, you might say. It's not just a different set of glasses that each culture wears. In a way, how people look at life becomes a sort of spirit which lives on even after their society has died."

Even though the patio was dark, I could tell he was staring deeply into my eyes. He continued. "Because my

27

theory is this. A spirit of a culture never dies once it has been given life. All it needs is someone who seeks to understand it, and it will return."

"You mean, like the spirit of the Romans lives on long after the fall of the empire?"

He relaxed and the tension in the air seemed to ease. "Good example. The Roman civilization was a great one indeed, contributing much to our lives today. And even the language of this culture—Latin—continues to live on, if only in the written form. Language is a powerful tool that the spirit of the cultures uses."

I didn't like the eerie feeling I had when he said "spirit." And I was skeptical. Perhaps he meant it as a metaphor. "You make it sound as if this spirit of culture is some sort of ghost or something. If it is so strong that it lives on forever, then why do empires crumble? They should live forever, too."

"Ah, but the crumbling proves that the spirits do exist. Societies fall apart because people begin to disregard their life views. They become lazy and indulgent, and don't protect their ideas from being corrupted. It's only natural that the spirit of the Romans wanted to destroy the people who had created it in order to shield itself from corruption."

"I don't know." I shook my head. Some of what he said sounded reasonable, and some of it bizarre. "You're saying that's what happened to the Caddoes. Then is that the reason you think that they were protesting—because they were being prompted by the Spirit of the Caddoes?" Somehow, this was all a little too mystical for me.

"It's possible. Did you know that there are still people who call themselves Druids living and practicing in England? Druids have existed since before recorded history in that country. What do you think draws modern people to ancient beliefs? All around the world—in South and Central America, in Africa, in Australia and China—people are interested in preserving old beliefs for future generations. It's happening in this country with the Christian fundamentalism and the various Native American faiths. Islamic fundamentalists are taking control in more and more Arabic countries.

"Why is all this happening? Have we become too civilized? Do people everywhere sense that they must prevent a global destruction of civilization by turning back to the old faiths? I don't know."

The stars flickered in the clear sky, much like the candles in their buckets. The world seemed ageless yet old, mysterious but ordinary. Somewhere in his words, I began to understand, or think that I understood. Could it be that there was some Spirit of the Caddoes, born eons ago, that still called to its people? An image of a streaked, shadowed face filled my mind. Was that man on the mound a worshiper of ancient spirits? Was he one of those who had protested? There was something vaguely familiar about the image. Maybe my mind turned too frequently to the spot on my brain where it had been burned in. Did Mother and I interrupt a sacred ritual, forcing him to attack us?

"I'd like to know more about the Caddo beliefs," I said quietly to the sky. Dr. Broussard's idea began to appeal to me, but I had always been a skeptic. Even so, the culture intrigued me.

I didn't want to seem too interested, though, because I wasn't sure I wanted to become involved with weird cults. And yet, if it had something to do with the Caddoes, it could help me in class, even make the excavation more interesting. After all, this was the Dean of Social Sciences.

"If you are really that interested, I know someone who could better answer your questions," he said softly. Anybody he recommended would probably be very knowledgeable.

I pushed my long hair up off my perspiring neck. "Who did you have in mind?"

"Oh, in my folklore collecting rounds I met an old Caddo woman who moved off the reservation many years ago to come back to East Texas where her ancestors lived. She's a shaman—a combination of priestess and herbal doctor. She doesn't accept visitors very often since she's suspicious of strangers. But if you are interested, I can make the arrangements. Just let me know."

I couldn't decide whether or not to go. It sounded strange and a bit scary. But I was letting my imagination run away with me again. I finally decided I'd go as a scientist for the archaeology class. "Ok."

Without another word, he stood and walked into the house.

I remained seated and waited for him to return. After twenty minutes, I realized he wasn't going to come back. My eyes fell on a candle nearest me. I watched its mesmerizing flame and couldn't shake a growing fear. There was an odd circle of evilness that was drawing me, and I was going willingly.

I only hoped I wouldn't be sucked in over my head.

Four

Nervously, I chose a seat in the middle of the classroom. There were a few quiet conversations between students, but the rest kept a watchful eye on the door.

At eleven o'clock, Dr. Petersen stepped into the room wearing a short-sleeved dress shirt with tie and khaki pants. He went directly to the board and wrote, "Arch. 201."

"I assume all of you have found your way to the right room," he said. He paused as another student found his way to the back of the class.

"I'm Dr. Petersen, and I'll be directing the excavation of the Caddo site. By the way, you'll note I said 'excavation,' not 'dig.' 'Digging' is done with a shovel. 'Excavating' means quite a bit more. We'll get into that later."

"Excavation," I scribbled, "NOT dig."

"Most of you are probably aware of the Indiana Jones image of archaeology. You see yourself courageously risking your life down some dark mine shaft, and being rewarded with a king's ransom in forgotten treasure—narrowly escaping death and personal injury, of course." He posed theatrically.

All of us laughed.

"If that's what you are looking for in this course, you

will be quite disappointed. You'll find I wear base-ball caps at site, not a felt fedora." Several students straightened their shoulders and arched their eyebrows. Naturally, they had not been so naive.

"This is a field course, and we will spend most of our time in the field. That means long hours in the hot sun patiently removing thin layer after thin layer of dirt. It means precise notes on every step of the excavation. And it means days—even weeks—of this before you uncover anything, if you uncover anything at all. You may only find a broken pottery sherd." We were quiet.

At this point, he handed out a sheet with the course requirements: Understand the history of the Caddo people in East Texas; keep daily excavation notes; under-stand the use of a grid at an archaeological site. . . . I gulped as I read down the list of twenty-three items. Had I made a mistake? This class looked too hard.

Twenty minutes into the lecture, someone made a commotion at the door. I turned, only to roll my eyes. Erica Petersen stood there with a half smile on her face. She juggled a load of books while the class stared at her. I could tell it was all an act.

"Is this Archaeology 201?" she asked her father sweet-ly, as if she didn't know him. I was going to be sick.

"Yes." Dr. Petersen frowned.

"Good!" She patiently scanned the rows until she found me. She granted me one of her smirks, and then her blue eyes gazed past. She lifted her books to one side, revealing the low V-cut hot pink blouse and her bare waist. Apparently spotting what she was looking for, she smiled warmly. "There's a seat back there."

Everyone I could see turned to follow her, especially the guys. She swept down my row, bumped my arm, and settled into a seat next to a handsome, athletic-looking guy at the back.

"Here, let me help you," the guy said, reaching for her books.

Dr. Petersen's lips were clamped in a tight line. "Young lady, should another juvenile compulsion for attention overcome you, I'd be happy to help you enroll in one of the elementary ed classes."

Everyone laughed and turned to see Erica. She got out her pen and notebook and appeared not to notice, but her cheeks were red. I couldn't come up with even a bit of pity for her.

During the rest of the class, Dr. Petersen gave a rough history of the Caddoes up to the time the site was built. He showed slides of the burial and temple mounds, and the house sites. He pointed out how the grid would be laid out.

As I jotted notes, I became fascinated by the Caddo people. At birth, they wrapped their babies' heads with a tight cloth, causing their long skulls. They decorated themselves with tattoos all over their bodies and painted themselves for special occasions. They lived in round grass huts and built larger huts on raised mounds as temples.

He ended the lecture. "Don't forget your sack lunch. The bus leaves at 7:00 A.M. sharp. Class dismissed." He picked up his notes and left the room.

Now that I knew how hard the course would be, I could have kicked myself for getting into it. What in the world did this have to do with my attacker? That incident had grown dim. I saw a long, hard summer ahead, instead of the fun I had hoped for. I gathered my things together.

As I stood in the aisle, someone bumped into me. I grasped the chair for balance. My hands released my notebook and purse, both of which opened and scattered under the next few rows of chairs.

I looked up, expecting an "excuse me," but only saw the swishing yellow hair of the girl I was growing to hate. She caught up with the muscular young man, batted her eyes, and surrendered her books to his arms.

As she stepped out the door with him, she cast me a hateful smile, then disappeared. I hopped over the desk in the now empty classroom and angrily gathered my belongings.

I stomped down the stairs instead of taking the elevator, banged open the main door of the Social Sciences Building, and charged straight to the bike rack. As I dug in my backpack for the key to the lock, someone whistled suggestively at me. I refused to turn around, though I wanted to punch the guy's lights out.

"Hey, Callie. Aren't you even going to say hello?"

Bart stood grinning near the building door. I blushed, both in pleasure and shame. His dark legs and arms bulged with muscles. White skin peeked from underneath his shirt sleeve. He hadn't gotten his tan at a pool like most of the guys in my high school. My mouth looked sour in his mirrored glasses, so I brightened my face with a smile.

"Hi. Where are you going?"

"I'm going to see if Dad wants to eat lunch with me. Once he starts the excavation, we won't have much time together."

"That's nice. Do you two do this often?" I envied any kid who enjoyed spending time with his parents. My parents and I had never had a just-for-fun lunch.

He shrugged. "We try to. Dad and I are alike. We both tend to do things in our own ways. And we enjoy being together occasionally without Mom and Erica around."

If his mom was anything like Erica, I could easily understand. "Well, I hope you guys have a nice lunch."

He didn't turn to go. "Say, how was the class?"

"Interesting." I shook my head. "No, scary. I think it will be a challenging summer, to say the least. He expects a lot from his students. I'm a little concerned that it will be too hard."

"Don't worry. His students always love this field class.

34

And he'll help you if you need it. You know, he wouldn't have let you in if he didn't think you could do it."

"Thanks." But inside, I was afraid I'd blow it.

I expected him to leave, but he hesitated, shifting his weight from one sneakered foot to another. "Hey, why don't you come and have lunch with us. That way, if Dad's too busy, I'll have someone to eat with."

It wasn't the best invitation I had ever received. Still, I wanted to go. Frankie's words came back to me about trusting myself, that I had good instincts. Come on, Callie. Eating a hamburger with a guy isn't going to kill you. He's nice enough. And it's not a "relationship," anyway.

"Ok," I heard myself say. I followed him back inside to the third floor office where his father was arranging books on his shelves.

Dr. Petersen seemed pleased with his son's suggestion. He winked at me when he said lunch was on him.

"Oh, no," groaned Bart. "That means cafeteria food again. The faculty has a discount at the slop line."

His father laughed. "Ok, ok! Actually, I thought we might hit Tom's Pizza. They have an 'all you can eat' special today. Believe me, Callie, they don't make any money off Bart."

Bart rolled his eyes and turned away from his dad. His face was red. "Parents. And they say children always say embarrassing things." I laughed, and was glad that Bart seemed to team with me.

Dr. Petersen locked his office, told his secretary he was leaving, and led the way across College Street to Tom's.

Over lunch I learned that Bart had started his own business doing odd jobs around town: everything from roof repair and house painting to mowing lawns and picking up trash. When the job was too big for him, he hired a few of his friends to help. Bart had the guts to make his own work instead of taking a job as a grocery

35

sacker. His dad was proud of him, as Bart was of his father.

When I relaxed some, I finally turned and looked at his handsome face. I enjoyed watching them joke back and forth. It was clear that they not only loved but also respected each other.

We were waiting for the check when one of Dr. Petersen's graduate students, the guy on the other side of the bushes at the picnic, rushed over to our table.

"The lab's been broken into," he blurted. "It's pretty messed up. Drawers are open and spilled onto the floor. A case of beakers was broken and thrown about the room. I don't know how the instruments or specimens are. Karen's checking on that now."

Dr. Petersen threw a wad of bills on the table and jumped up to go. Bart and I followed them out the door and across campus, having to run to keep up with them.

On the second floor of the Social Sciences building, University Police already stood at the door of the lab. Dr. Petersen elbowed his way past them with us close behind. As Dale, the graduate student, had described, the room lay covered—shelves, counters and floor—with broken glass. Someone had pelted bottles into every corner of the room. The sight sickened me. The other graduate student, Karen, had swept away the glass in one area and was putting things back into a drawer.

As I turned, my eye caught a flash of red on the pale green cinder block wall through which we had entered the lab. Dripping, bloody letters spelled: "BEWARE THE CADDO ANIMUS!" My heart raced as the now familiar fear returned. Indian, Caddo, spirit, attacker—I didn't understand why these people, or whoever, should want to hurt any of us. Once again, I pictured the shadowy face with his hand reaching toward my throat.

I must have gasped, because Dr. Petersen whirled

around. He crossed to the wall and touched the wet-looking letters. "It's dry."

"It's not blood . . ."

"No, it's just glossy paint, and damn hard to get off."

The female officer tapped his shoulder. "Excuse me, Dr. Petersen, but we need to get a statement. Your assistant, Karen, tells us that she and Dale were in here yesterday afternoon and left after locking the door around 5:00 P.M. She said she came back at noon today, unlocked the door, and found it like this. Were you in here between those times? We're trying to pin down when this happened."

"No, the last I saw it was just before they closed up last night. I locked my office, then we all left together to go to the faculty picnic. Did you check the lock?"

The police woman nodded. "It doesn't appear to have been tampered with. Who else would have keys to this lab?"

Dr. Petersen raised his eyebrows. "Well, lots of people, come to think of it, but none who shouldn't have them. You guys, of course. And the Maintenance Department would have some. Karen, Dale, and I are the only ones who have keys checked out to this room. I think the Department has a couple of spares. You'd have to ask the secretary where she keeps them. If anyone wanted to get in here with a key, there would be all sorts of places to get one."

She didn't reply, but jotted something in her notebook. "Do you know any reason why someone would do this?"

He shrugged and looked at the mess. "Who knows? To get revenge for some imagined wrong I did them. To ruin my reputation. To stop the excavation—everyone knows that it's something I've been working toward for years. Or maybe some student wants to spread rumors that the Caddo spirits are still alive just to make the summer more interesting. There could be reasons that I can't even think of."

"You said someone might want to get revenge. Did you have anyone in mind? Do you have enemies that might do this to you?"

He shook his head. "Enemies? Not that I know of. Rivals? Sure. You ought to know that there are always rivalries—usually several—in every department. What I had in mind was an angry student: one who needed an A but got a B, or one who needed to pass but failed. Every professor has heard horror stories of the bitter student turned vicious. We all laugh at it, but it has an uncomfortable ring of truth."

The officer smiled wryly. "So what do you make of the graffiti?"

I followed their eyes back to the hastily scrawled letters.

"I don't know," he reflected. "It's spelled correctly, so it wasn't a freshman."

Everyone laughed, and the tension eased.

"I think it was written by a frat rat who couldn't spell animal," Karen quipped, and we laughed again.

The officer had the patient smile of someone who regularly had to deal with professors.

What did Dr. Broussard say? "The spirit of the Caddoes lives on after the people have died," I said, and Dr. Petersen looked at me, startled. Then he slowly nodded and turned back to the letters.

He leaned back on a black lab table. "You're right, Callie. 'Animus' comes from Jungian psychology. It can mean governing spirit or basic attitude. It can also mean an evil will. I would assume here it could read 'beware of angry Caddo spirits.' We'll be digging up a sacred burial ground, you know."

I shivered. I certainly didn't want to be the object of revenge by angry ghosts.

The officer looked closely at him. "So you wouldn't

38

rule out those young Caddoes who were on campus protesting?"

"I guess not. I hadn't thought them capable of something like this, but anything's possible. Maybe I haven't taken them as seriously as I should."

Images flashed through my mind: I saw a figure on a hill with its arms stretched toward the moon, a snarling face in a dark car window, and the profile of a young, handsome Indian firmly proclaiming, "We'll be back." I wanted to be fair, but I couldn't help but wonder once again if they were linked. Or was all this caused by evil spirits?

The officer said, "We'll need a full damage report as soon as possible. Notify me at once if you think there is something stolen. Karen says that it seems to be only minor damage, but you'll need to make a complete list, ok?"

"Fine. If all of us chip in," he gave Bart and me a pleading look and we nodded, "we can probably have this place straightened and the list ready this afternoon. And then, of course, we have to prepare for the field tomorrow."

As Dr. Petersen walked the officers down to the main Social Sciences office, Dale joined Karen in straightening overturned drawers. Bart grabbed the broom and I took a whisk broom and dust pan to begin cleaning the counters.

As I swept the glass into small piles, I dreaded what surprises might be in store tomorrow at the site.

Five

The surprise was a thunderstorm that had moved in during the night. I awoke at six, turned off my alarm and swept open the curtain. Gusts of wind blew the heavy rain hard against my window. Lightning flashed.

I flicked on my portable radio and found a weather report. "Flash flood warnings are in effect for all of eastern Texas and western Louisiana, with a 70 percent chance of thunder showers continuing until late tonight. Today's high should reach 78 with an overnight low of 72. Tomorrow, clearing skies with a high of . . ." I turned it off and pulled on denim shorts and a white blouse.

In the kitchen, I started a pot of coffee, then opened the pantry to study the cereal selection. The front door slammed. A gust of cool air drifted over to me. Dr. Broussard, dressed in a soaked brown robe and pajamas, rushed in holding a dripping newspaper out in front of him with one hand cupped underneath.

"Morning, Callie." He tossed the paper into the sink. "Wish we could have had some rain today. It sure is dry." He chuckled at his joke.

I smiled and grabbed a wad of paper towels to wipe up his puddles. "I guess the summer monsoons are here."

"Yeah." He separated the soggy plastic sack from the wet newsprint. "June always seems to bring a lively

40

weather show. 'Scuse me." He wiggled past and flung the limp roll into the oven. He winked as he turned the dial. "This always dries it out."

"Want some coffee? It's about done."

"What a perfect house guest! Cleans up my drips and makes coffee, too. From underneath the covers, I heard Frankie grumbling about having to wake up. She should be in soon."

We sat at the linoleum table sipping our coffee. "I guess my field trip is canceled."

He nodded. "Yeah. You know, there is a stream running through the site. Even if you kids weren't struck by lightning, you could be caught in a flash flood. Besides, you couldn't do anything in this mess."

"I know, but I was looking forward to it."

He gave me a fatherly smile. "Look at it this way. The ground will be soft tomorrow making the digging easier. It's probably the best thing that could have happened." He hesitated. "Besides, I made an appointment for you today."

I looked at him blankly. "Appointment?"

He cleared his throat, apparently not sure of continuing. "We were talking about that Caddo shaman the other night. I bumped into her at the gas station yesterday and told her about you. It was odd. She seemed to have been waiting there for me. And when I said you were interested in seeing her, she said, 'Tomorrow. I'll see her tomorrow.' Then she drove off. I didn't have a chance to tell her you would be out at the site all day." He looked out the kitchen window at the storm-tossed trees.

That's strange, I thought. I eyed him to see if he was playing a joke on me. "I guess she knew about the weather report," I said.

He shook his head and lowered his eyebrows in thought. "She doesn't own a TV or radio. There isn't even a radio in her car. She says it interferes with her ability to listen to the spirits."

Part of me was intrigued, and the other part argued that this was a bunch of bull. I tried to think of an excuse not to go. But on the other hand, the woman sounded fascinating. "I guess I don't have anything else to do."

He took a pad and pencil and wrote down the directions. He handed them to me. "Her name is Manitu Flying Eagle. You'll see her cabin where I've marked it on the map. Don't expect anything fancy. She doesn't like modern conveniences."

"When does she expect me?" The question sounded melodramatic to my ears and made me feel self-conscious, again.

He shrugged and half-smiled. "I guess she knows when."

Frankie appeared at the door wrapped in a black and white kimono, her hair pressed up on one side from sleep. "She knows when what?" She yawned largely.

Dr. Broussard rocked back in his padded plastic chair and puckered for a kiss. "She knows when the coffee is made. You have an incredible nose, my love!"

She relaxed her upper body and half fell toward his mouth, putting on the brakes just in time to prevent lip injury. "Smelling coffee is a delightful way to wake up," she mumbled while her lips still rested on his. "Good morning, Callie."

After eating a large breakfast, Dr. Broussard took his now dry newspaper with him to dress. Before Frankie and I had finished the last bit of coffee, he left for work.

The sky had turned a slightly lighter shade of gray, but the sun didn't stand a chance with those thunderheads. I stood by the sliding glass doors in the living room and pressed my nose against the cool surface. The play of droplets on the glass hypnotized me.

"Callie?" I turned to see Frankie dressed for work. Her earth-mama style clothes looked beautiful on her. "Why don't you give Bart a call? He can't possibly be doing any work today. Maybe the two of you could find something interesting to do. Otherwise, you'll be stuck here without a car, unless you want to ride to the University with me."

I loved how Frankie's musical voice expressed genuine concern for me. It wasn't at all like Mother's pinched, blaming sounds.

"That's not a bad idea. I like Bart."

"Good. I think I'd like him, too, if I got to know him. Oh, and I've given the University a call, and they confirm that the excavation has been canceled for today."

"Thanks, Frankie."

"No problem. And listen, if you two go out, be careful. This area is prone to flash flooding. But then you're old enough to use your head." Once again with Frankie, I felt a rush of self-confidence—more than I had felt in a long time. Frankie's trust in me was nice—very nice.

She left through the garage door. As I heard the Toyota's engine, the phone rang. On the other end, Bart sounded grumpy.

"I've just got to get out of this house. Erica's driving me nuts. Mind if I come over?"

"No, but I have some place I want to go."

"Tell me about it when I arrive, and I'll drive you. Ok?"

"That would be great." I liked the idea of having someone else go with me to see the Caddo woman, but I worried about what he might think of the idea.

When he arrived, he dashed from his pickup to the house wearing a long orange poncho. He slid the dripping plastic off in the hallway and handed me a small orange packet.

"What's this?"

"Your poncho. I figured a city girl wouldn't have the sense to bring proper rain gear for East Texas. An umbrella isn't much use against rain that blows sideways."

"Thanks. It's, uh, lovely."

"It will keep you dry. So where are we off to? Bart's taxi, at your service."

I took a big breath. "You're going to think I'm crazy, but I want to see a woman who might have some answers about the threats your father is receiving. At least she can explain something about the Caddoes to us." I told him what Dr. Broussard said the other night and this morning. "So it looks like this woman knew that I would be available today. I suppose she could have listened to the weather report, but I think it's worth checking out."

Bart was quiet a moment. "Dr. Broussard said she was a shaman? He knows the real meaning of the word. He wouldn't toss it around lightly. If it had been my mother or sister, I wouldn't pay any attention. They occasionally go to Sister Navajo for their astrological charts. Dad has checked her out and found that she's a phony, but they won't hear it. They pay money for predictions that could apply to anybody."

"So you haven't heard of Manitu Flying Eagle?" I frowned. "Maybe that's not a good sign. Your mom and sister would have heard of her."

Bart shook his blond head. "No, I don't think so. Dr. Broussard said she didn't like modern conveniences. That means she probably wouldn't advertise herself like Sister Navajo does."

"She thinks that the people who should come to her will find her on their own? How would she earn a living?"

He shrugged. "I've heard that all pure-blood Indians receive government money. Maybe she gets something like that. Or maybe she lives off the land."

I stuffed some money in my pocket in case she was more profit minded than Bart thought. He helped me put on the poncho in the entrance hall, where he was still dripping. I locked the front door and we dashed to the truck through the pelting rain.

44

From behind the wheel, Bart studied the map, switched his truck into four wheel drive, and we were off. Wide streams of gray water flowed downhill at the edges of the streets, leaving only a single lane in the center. We passed several stalled cars and tow trucks in low areas. Were we foolish to be out? It seemed even sillier to go to a medicine woman or whatever she was.

"Bart, maybe it isn't safe to go today. I don't want your truck to get stuck."

He waved his hand. "Don't worry about it. I've got a winch on the back. And the four wheel drive will take us through anything. When you drive off-road in East Texas, you have to be able to go through a lot of mud." He turned to me with a kind look on his face. "Don't worry. We'll see her together."

"Thanks," I said, and relaxed a little.

We drove silently for most of the way, each of us with an eye on the clouds. The lightning crackled more closely. I was glad when we drove into the tall pine forest. At least the trees had a better chance of being hit. When the sky became greenish, I twisted to watch for funnel clouds.

At last Bart turned onto a logging road. The truck gripped the slippery red clay as if it were gravel. About a half mile down on the left, just where Dr. Broussard had marked on the map, was a log cabin nestled in a small clearing. Bart turned in and stopped the engine.

Rain poured down the windshield now that the wipers lay still. The cabin looked empty and had no curtains on the dirty windows. We could see no car, though Bart spotted some fresh tire tracks.

"Well, shall we go in?"

"I don't know," I began, when I saw a hand place a candle in one window. "I guess that means yes."

We slammed the doors shut and pulled the poncho hoods down over our faces as we ran to the porch. On one side of the door, a strip of wood was attached to the wall with nails pegged into it every few inches. We hung our dripping plastic there.

The door swung open of its own accord just like a real spook house. With a quick glance at each other, we stepped in.

"Hello?" I called. "I'm Callie Davis. Dr. Broussard sent me."

"No, he did not send you. I sent for you."

The deep, craggy voice came from the opposite corner of the dark. I stared in that direction. Someone in a cloak sat at a table facing the door.

"Come in, close the door, and sit. The wind chills me," the low gruff voice commanded.

We shut the door and stumbled across the irregular floor to the two wooden chairs in front of the table. We sat down.

"I'm . . ." Bart began.

"I know who you are, Bart Petersen, better than you know yourself. I will speak some to you today. But it is with this girl that the spirits desire to communicate, if she is willing. I will help if I can, but a seed cannot grow on infertile ground."

She clicked her thick fingers and candles flared around the room. I gasped with uneasy surprise and looked back at her. The tan Indian blanket heavily shadowed her face revealing only her sharp, unfeminine chin. A feeling of deja vu swept over me.

"What did you want to see me about?" I finally managed.

"Sssh," she commanded. She withdrew an intricately carved wooden pipe from one of the folds of the blanket. Feathers were attached underneath the stone bowl. She chanted words from a strange language as she withdrew something from a pouch. She lit it, and puffed on the pipe a few times. The leaves she had placed in the bowl were definitely not ordinary tobacco, but it wasn't pot, either.

46

She handed it stiffly toward me. "Uh, no thank you, I don't smoke."

She thrust it at me again. "Tobacco is sacred. Smoke!"

I glanced at Bart and took the pipe. The harsh smoke made me cough. Still coughing, I handed the pipe back to her, but she wouldn't take it.

"Again," she barked.

I couldn't decide if this were some sort of ritual or if she intended harm. To be on the safe side, I didn't suck much this time, and managed not to cough. With her hand she indicated that I should pass it to Bart. He puffed a few times without coughing, and handed it back to her. She again drew the smoke into her lungs, then placed the pipe on the table. The pungent smoke filled the room.

"The spirit of smoke binds our souls together. Now we may seek understanding. Callie, the unbeliever, you are in danger. So that you may open your eyes to the truth, the spirits have shown me the fierce anger you have for your mother. Underneath this fire lies the pain of her neglect of you when you needed her. But your heart will heal, and the anger will melt."

My mouth fell open. "I can't believe it! How can you—?"

"Silence, fool girl. The spirits have chosen you, though their ways sometimes surpass my understanding. I tell you again, you are in danger. These are not tricks for your amusement.

"I understand now why they chose the cards to carry their message to you. You, who are too ignorant to understand. You must listen with your heart, not your head." She shook her head, as if still amazed that she was to communicate things to me, of all people. I felt stupid and unworthy, and that I should try hard to please her.

Again, her deep voice began a quiet song and her large hands motioned in the air over the table. From another fold she brought forth a thick deck of cards with intricate Native American symbols on the back. Her song rose in intensity as she shuffled the deck about, then laid it on the table in front of her. In rapid succession, she placed five cards face down in the shape of a pyramid in front of her. Holding a rough hand above each one, she sung a phrase and then flipped it over. When they were all facing up, she stopped singing.

She looked up toward me, and though I couldn't make out her face, I could see her eyes glinting yellow from reflected candlelight. "Here is what the spirits would say to you."

She showed me the first card which pictured a wolf howling at three phases of the moon. "Danger is implied by the wolf, and you can see the dark-face, half-face, and full-face moons. It means you are on the threshold of life and death."

On the next, an Indian brave with one leg tied to a stake fought off an enemy. "Bravery is a quality much admired by my people. In times past, some warriors would tether themselves during battle to prevent a retreat, and thus show a supreme level of confidence in their skills and understanding of their enemies' ways of war. The card says that you will need knowledge of human nature and perseverance, and these will bring you success."

Perhaps she was right to call me ignorant, because I didn't have the faintest idea of what she was trying to tell me. It all seemed like a foreign language I didn't know, but wanted to.

The third showed an Indian stealing a horse. "The horse brought freedom to Native Americans, and was considered a treasure. Since the white man was an intruder, it was both dangerous and honorable to take his horses. You will see your ends achieved, but only after undergoing danger. You must persevere and stay confident in yourself."

I looked more closely at the card and wondered at what she saw in it. Confident in myself, just like Frankie said. Did all shamans speak in riddles?

She paused before going onto the next cards. "These are the forces you must avoid." The first card was turned upside-down, facing Bart and me: a chief paddled at the head of a canoe.

"This card is reversed and so has the opposite meaning of what is pictured. A man is your enemy. He is amazingly crafty, and conceals his violence. Underneath his calm surface, he wants your blood. He is ruthless and has no conscience. He is a very dangerous enemy, Callie."

Despite my attempts at rational calm, my body became rigid. My heart pounded in my throat as the image in the car window again appeared in my mind. I grabbed Bart's hand. Everything this strange woman was saying had an uncanny ring of truth to it, though I couldn't explain why, just as I couldn't explain my sudden panic.

With horror I looked back to the table and the last card. A warrior lay dead in a desert with three arrows sticking in his back.

"This is Ruin," she said ominously. "Your downfall will be brought on by rash actions, so you must use your head. You must beware of your friends as well as your enemies."

She passed her hands over the tops of the cards and began to sing again. As before, her words became louder, then stopped abruptly. She folded her hands in her lap and raised her head to me.

"Here is the meaning. You are in danger. You and others could be called to leave this world forever and walk in the spirit world. No matter how tough it becomes, you must keep striving bravely to defeat your enemy. Watch all around you, for here is where your enemy hides. You must be smarter than your crafty adversary, or you will die. He is a chameleon and will show you

49

only his brighter side. But every animal leaves marks when it passes. Hunt for his."

"You can see all that in those cards?" Bart looked suspicious.

She didn't reply.

Part of me felt truth in her words, yet another part was wary. I was puzzled. "You keep referring to the enemy as 'he.' Could it be a she?"

"It is the same." Now I really didn't know what to think.

The room seemed stuffy. I wanted to leave. I wasn't sure whether I trusted this woman or not. I let go of Bart's hand and reached for some money in my pocket. "How much do I owe you?"

She screeched, sending chills through my gut. "Unbeliever! It is as I said, no? Go away. I don't want to be contaminated by your green filth. Leave, I say. LEAVE."

She stood up quickly, grabbed the pipe and lunged for me. We didn't need further encouragement. We ran for the door, nabbed our ponchos, and dashed into the rain toward the truck.

As I opened the door on the passenger's side, I saw her huddling on the porch, still hidden in the Indian blanket.

"Young man," she called. "If this fool of a girl means anything to you, stick beside her."

We didn't wait for more advice. The doors slammed shut, the engine roared, and we pulled out as quickly as possible into the thick mud of the road.

Six

An eagle flew at me with talons stretched and beak open in a war cry. With feet frozen to the ground, I stood trembling atop a lone hill and batted it away, trying to shield my face and yet watch for its next attack.

The alarm buzzed next to my ear. I opened my eyes and slapped the button. A shudder went through me. The incredibly realistic nightmare reminded me of Manitu Flying Eagle. Don't think of it. It's only a dream.

I pictured the ride home from the shaman's hut; the rain lessened as Bart and I drove farther away, as if the storm had been centered over that clearing in the woods where Manitu made her home.

Bart and I had discussed what she had said, what she might have meant.

"We have to take what she said with a grain of salt," I told him as we sat in his truck outside of Frankie's house.

"That's an understatement," he snorted. "But I guess it won't hurt to keep a watchful eye on things around us. The way Dad's lab was trashed shows that."

Bart pulled into Frankie's driveway and turned off the engine. As it was still raining steadily, though not the gully washer of an hour before, I struggled to put on the wet poncho before dashing to the house.

"Here, let me help you." I raised my arms over my head and groped for the collar.

And then we were nose to nose. Our lips touched, then met again. I broke it off. I quickly mumbled good-bye and ran inside the house.

I shook the images from my head and glanced at the digital clock on the headboard: 6:22 A.M. I'd have to hurry to catch the bus for the field site.

The cool damp morning air flowed past me as I biked to campus. Sleepy red sunlight bathed the quiet town. I coasted down a long winding hill on a residential street, listening to dogs barking in backyards.

The parking lot behind the Social Sciences building was nearly empty. A few students already stood at the bus stop. I rode the bike over the sloping curve to the bike rack, parked and locked it there.

When I reached the students, I said good morning. The guy next to me turned, and I saw it was the same one Erica had been flirting with on the first day of class. He had on Weches State Athletics shirt and shorts. He had to be on an athletic scholarship.

"Hi," he said. "Are you ready for this? I hope Petersen doesn't grade too hard, because I'm counting on this course to bring up my average. Hey, you didn't buy an extra field notebook, did you? I forgot to get one."

I shook my head. "Sorry."

"That's ok. We probably won't need them today."

I stifled the urge to shake my head.

A yellow school bus drove into the parking lot followed by a white car. The bus stopped in front of us and the driver opened the door.

"This is for Archaeology 201," the driver called.

I felt an elbow in my ribs. "By the way, which dorm are you living in? Oh, yeah. I'm Nick Jackson."

"Callie Davis. And I don't live on campus." That was as much information as I was going to give him.

From around the front of the bus, Erica and Dr. Petersen

appeared. Erica scanned the crowd and saw me just as Nick suggested I should go ahead of him up the bus stairs. She flushed as if outraged.

As we walked down the aisle, he pointed to a seat on his right. "This looks like a good place." He smiled as if I ought to sit with him.

I was tempted to have a seat just to irritate Erica. But encouraging him would probably lead to helping him with his homework. "You go ahead," I said, and chose a seat further down.

Erica had been watching the whole thing. With a haughty look and a swish of her bottom, she said loudly, "Oh, hi, Nick! Were you saving this seat for me, you sweet thing?" She settled into the bench, fluffed her blond locks so they hung over the back and turned to him, batting her color-caked eyes.

Disgusting. I stared out the window.

Thirty minutes later the bus pulled up to the site, passing the Restricted Area sign nailed to a pine tree. We stopped at a clearing. Under Dr. Petersen's orders, we emptied the bus but stayed in a group.

After a lecture about the day's plans, he led the class to the stake which would be the datum point for the site's grid. Karen and Dale showed how the first few strings and stakes would be laid. We awkwardly followed their example, and soon the area looked like a giant piece of graph paper with lines running north/south and east/west, squares one meter in size.

Every spot in the meadow had a student bending, measuring, hammering stakes or stretching string. As the day heated up, the dampness in the ground began to evaporate, bathing us in steam. Finally, we retreated to the shade for lunch.

After we had eaten, we were lectured on the importance of accurate maps of the area. Topographic maps were passed out and we located the site on each. During the afternoon we sketched the grid and included trees,

53

the stream running across the property and large rocks. Karen and Dale gathered us together and showed us the tools.

At four o'clock, almost everyone was in the shade instead of under the sun. But Dr. Petersen coaxed us out again with the assignment of squares. He indicated where likely houses had been built, where temple and burial mounds were. He passed around a grid map with many squares colored. These had priority. With a class list in hand, he began randomly calling names, asking which site each student would like to work.

While waiting for my name, I carefully walked the grid looking for a spot that appealed to me. I came to the edge of the burial ground and kicked the dirt with my tennis-shoed foot. I scanned the weeds and stopped when I saw a bird feather propped up against a small rock. It was roughly six inches long and black and white.

"Davis, Callie. Which square?"

I glanced back to the datum point and counted the squares to the one with the feather. "Two north, five west."

Why did I pick that one? It wasn't even at the center of the mound, just on the edge. As I compared it to the squares around, this one had lusher grass. "What a reason for picking it! All I'm likely to find is a lot of dirt and clay," I muttered to myself.

After all the students had picked a spot, I walked up to Dale, who had the grid with each of our names.

"Say, Dale. I was wondering if I could change my square. I'm beginning to think I won't find anything there."

He laughed. "Lots of you won't find anything spectacular, but you'll all find something, no doubt."

"Would you mind if I take a look to see if a better spot is available?"

"Go ahead, but I doubt if you'll find anything better than what you have."

54

He was right. I took the grid to the field again and checked each spot. There was nothing better available.

"Cheer up," he said as I handed the sheet back to him. "These mounds have been here a long time. Remember that they were much larger once, but have been eroded over the centuries. Your spot is on the sloping part of ground, so it would have been in the middle of the original hill."

"I guess you're right." I didn't feel much better. It had been an impulsive choice.

Only a few students and I poked around the site, the rest waited in the shade. I climbed to the top of the burial mound and looked over the area. It was a large meadow with pine forest framing each side. We had been told that this section of the woods had been clear cut for the lumber, and that was how the site had been discovered several years ago. One of the lumberjacks, who had a sizable collection of Indian artifacts, noticed that the stream contained pottery shards and contacted the University.

As I stood there, a strange feeling came over me. I felt as if someone were watching me from the woods on the opposite side. The branches on a clump of bushes seemed to move, then were still. I shivered and quickly joined the rest.

By sunset, our stomachs were growling and the water jugs were running low. There was still no sign of the bus.

"I don't like this. The bus is over an hour and a half late," I heard Dale say in a low voice to Karen.

"Perhaps it broke down. Most of the University buses are old," she replied.

"Maybe it did break down. And maybe someone helped it along."

She arched her eyebrows, still looking at the dirt, but didn't speak.

The students became noisy and restless. They talked and laughed in groups, but several said loudly that they might hitchhike back to campus because they hadn't brought along sleeping bags for a camp-out.

I glanced around the group. Dr. Petersen and an African student in colorful traditional dress were having a serious conversation. Someone had brought a Frisbee and several guys tossed it back and forth. God only knew where they got the energy. Erica and Nick sat on a log making eyes at each other, exchanging whispers and giggling.

From around the bend in the road, we heard the sound of an engine and a chassis banging and squeaking. Several of us stood expectantly, only to be disappointed when a pick-up truck came into view. It was Bart.

We gathered around him as he opened the door and stood on the frame. "Well, I've got some good news and bad news, folks. I was waiting at the bus stop for about thirty minutes when your bus driver got out of a car. Apparently, he had driven just a few miles out of town when the clutch broke. So he hitched back to the school to pick up another bus and call a wrecker. I drove him to the bus barn, where I left him, but he wasn't able to find the manager with the keys to the office. So I stopped by the University Police Department, and they're on their way to let him in. He'll have to put gas in another one before he heads this way, so it could be a while."

At this everyone groaned.

"Now the good news. I can take a lot of you back with me, if you're willing to ride in the back."

"I'm so hungry, I'll hang on to the tail gate if you'll take me," one guy said, bringing chuckles from the rest.

"Yeah, I'll ride on the hood," another said.

Dr. Petersen spoke up. "We have to do this safely, or the University will have my neck. We can get three more in the cab and ten in the bed, but no more. The rest of us will have to wait for the bus. Any volunteers to stay besides Karen and Dale?" Those two rolled their eyes.

"It's one of the many benefits of being a lab assistant," he said to them with a smile.

They shrugged their shoulders in resignation, while the rest whistled and clapped.

"Any others?"

A quiet fell over the group. "Ok. I'll stay." I said, "Bart, will you call Frankie?"

With some prodding, Dr. Petersen eventually had enough volunteers. He told Erica to stay, and she pouted until Nick said he would wait for the bus, too. The sun was setting as the rest crowded onto the pickup. Bart reached into the glove compartment and handed his father the flashlight. "You might need this."

His father nodded. "Check at the bus barn. If he hasn't left yet, send somebody after us, ok?"

Bart looked at me thoughtfully, then slowly smiled. "I'll come myself."

The forest grew considerably quieter as the truck engine faded in the distance. I went to the clearing and looked up at the sky. A few stars had appeared in the twilight. A flicker of light caught my attention. Far in the distance to my right a fire burned bright and tall. It was in the woods, and for a fearful moment, I thought a forest fire was beginning. But then I noticed that it died down and did not spread. Someone was camping and had just started their campfire.

I went back to tell the others.

"I didn't know that camping was allowed in this area," Dale said.

"It's not," Karen said flatly. "This is National Forest land, and no camping permits are allowed. But that won't stop those people who want to get back to nature."

"Yeah, but what they don't realize is that they are spoiling the unspoiled forest just by being there," he countered.

"All right, you two," Dr. Petersen warned. "I don't want another of your arguments now." He turned to the

57

rest of us. "You'll soon learn that Karen is our back-to-nature person, while Dale claims a more 'realistic' viewpoint. Spare us, please."

I went back to the edge of the meadow to watch the stars and to keep an eye on the campfire. Bull frogs began their heavy chorus accompanied by high cricket songs. An owl, a dark shape against the star-speckled sky, glided silently across the field, swooped down briefly, and flew away with a small object in its talons.

Faintly at first so that it blended in with the night sounds, another group of voices began chanting. As the sound grew louder and more clear, I could tell the voices were human and coming from the campfire area. The chant sounded menacing and evil, and I shivered. I gradually realized it was not in English, and didn't sound like any language I'd ever heard.

My heart beat in my throat and my arms sweated. I suppressed my instinct to run, hoping I could make out a figure against the firelight.

A twig snapped nearby. I wheeled around. Something whistled by my ear. I threw myself down. An object vibrated as it stuck in a tree trunk. Adrenalin shot my body onto its feet and through the woods to the others before my brain realized what happened. I saw the flashlight, picked out Dr. Petersen in the darkness, raced to him and grabbed his arm.

"Someone's out here," I panted. "They just threw something at me and barely missed my ear."

Before he could respond, the woods around us began echoing with a loud whisper: "Violators. Violators. You tread on holy ground, dirty Wasichu. We come back from the spirit world to protect our bones. We avenge our disturbed rest with your blood. Violators. Dirty Wasichu."

Who's out there, I wondered. Dr. Petersen turned off the flashlight and whispered that all of us should sit in a circle with our backs inward.

"Someone is playing a cruel prank," he told us quietly

as the loud rasping voice continued its accusations.

"But why would someone want you off this land so badly?" I asked. I crossed my legs on the ground, not sure whether I was glad to be sitting next to him or not if he might be the next target.

"In my country, men who are desperate try to have their way by using—how do you say—superstitions?" I turned my head and saw that it was the young African guy who spoke.

"That's true," Karen whispered. "But what could they want on this land so desperately?"

"Pre-Columbian artifacts bring a healthy price on the black market," Dale replied. "Greed could motivate someone to go to all this trouble."

I had a feeling money wasn't the motive. "Or fear. Maybe the pots are already gone. Maybe they're afraid of being caught."

Dr. Petersen spoke up. "There's almost no way to trace stolen artifacts. Anyone who knows anything about the market would know that. But it doesn't matter. They're not scaring me off."

Abruptly, the chanting stopped and the fire went out. If the whispering had frightened me, the sudden silence was worse. We froze as we waited for some telltale sign from the woods. What we would do if we were attacked? From time to time, someone very carefully shifted weight from one hip to another on the pine-needle-covered ground.

After a long time, we heard the sound of an engine in the distance, and I knew that Bart had returned. The headlights blinded us as he pulled up and jumped out.

"Hey, gang, how's the powwow? Did you have a fight, or is it part of the ceremony not to face each other?" His grin faded as he caught our solemn expressions. Dale described what had happened since Bart had left. Bart didn't speak but scanned the woods angrily.

"Well, it's time to go home everybody," Dr. Petersen said.

I could still hear in my mind the sound of an object swishing past my ear and my heart raced again. "I want to find what was thrown at me."

"You'll never find it tonight," Dale said almost condescendingly.

"We can try," Karen countered, heading toward the clearing. I reached for Dr. Petersen's flashlight and followed her. The others fell in behind.

As we reached the clearing, I found the spot where I had been standing, and we fannned out. "I heard a twig snap from that direction and it hit a tree over there."

We crawled through briar and brush and I moved the flashlight across the trees in front of us. A glint of light about eye level caught my eye. "There it is."

With some effort, I pulled a long hunting knife from the trunk. On its handle held with a leather thong were a feather, remarkably like the one on the square I had chosen, and a wilted plant.

Despite the heat of the evening, I felt cold.

Seven

The next day as we arrived back at the site, I was struck by what a contrast it was from last night. "What a difference daylight makes," I said to no one in particular. Fear wasn't going to get the best of me again.

In the morning lecture, Karen and Dale showed us how to begin digging our squares with a spade until we reached a paler layer of dirt. We were told to leave four-foot-wide "balks," or walls, between each of the squares. We would walk on these as the work progressed. Dale showed us how to check the straightness of the walls with a plumb bob so that we could measure the depth of each layer of dirt. This would help determine the age of the site. But he reminded us that we should leave any original dirt walls intact, whether they were straight or not.

Karen picked one student's square to use as an example. As the sun rose higher evaporating the dew on the wild grasses around us, we fidgeted, eager to start our own squares. With a few last words of instruction, we were released and the work began in earnest.

Why had I chosen my square? "I hope Dale's right," I muttered as I climbed to the top and watched everyone work. We looked like a colony of ants scurrying around the mounds. I walked down the other side, carefully stepping over crisscrossed strings and stakes until I reached my square.

The feather was gone. I don't know why I expected it to be there as if it were rooted in the dirt. The image of a feathered knife flashed through my head, and I shivered at the memory.

Something was going on that I couldn't explain. The face in the car window. The protesting Caddoes. Bloody threats on the lab wall. Manitu Flying Eagle's predictions. Campfires, chanting and a knife which narrowly missed me.

Flying Eagle. A feather on an Indian mound and on a knife. Was there a connection? Was Manitu trying to warn me of something? So many of the things she said seemed real. Did she have some sort of special power, or was I reading too much into this? Was it more than a hoax last night?

I squatted in the dirt and leaned on my spade letting my mind whirl. I hadn't seen those Caddoes for a while. What were they up to? They could have tried to scare us off. Was their leader such a fanatical believer that he would resort to violence to protect his buried ancestors? Maybe. But how could anyone understand someone else's motives after just one meeting?

"Davis, get to work."

I jumped. It was Dr. Petersen. He was looking at me with a patient smile.

"Sorry. So many confusing things have been happening. It's taken over my thoughts. I was trying to sort it out." I stopped apologizing, embarrassed that he found me sitting around when he had gone to so much trouble to put me in the class in the first place.

He put one hand on my shoulder. "That was a close call last night, wasn't it? I'm sorry. I'm sure it shook you up. I was so concerned with the safety of the group that I didn't stop to think how that attack must have affected you."

His concern felt nice, and needed. I envied Bart having such a caring father. "It's all right. I was so tired last night after such a long day that I fell asleep right away. I haven't thought much about it until now. I'm fine, really."

He squeezed my shoulder affectionately. "Back to work, then."

I watched him go and my eyes casually scanned the field. Erica was scowling. When she saw that I saw her, she turned her back to me. She flirted with Nick, whose square was next to hers. I picked up the spade, disgusted with her, not willing to watch her any more.

The edge of my shovel clinked against the rocky soil. Only a couple of inches of dirt came out at a time, which I dumped into an old green wheelbarrow. Before much of a dent had been made in my square, I carted the full wheelbarrow to the growing mound of dirt off-site. Now the field looked like a gopher town. Although the upper layer was still soft from the rain two days before, I found hard-packed red clay a few inches down.

When we stopped for lunch, the coolers of soft drinks were surrounded like a carcass with ravens. I stood behind Nick as he reached into the ice-filled container.

He looked back at me. "What can I hand you?" Ok, so he was nice.

"Oh, any diet drink will do." We popped the tops and drank deeply.

"So how's your square going?" he asked.

"I've hit clay. It's getting tough." My finger gently probed a blister on the palm of my hand.

He nodded. "I know. But there's a sandy layer below that. Just keep going and it will be easier. Do you understand how to write up the field notes for today?"

"I guess they'll tell us, but I think we write down how deep we've dug and what sort of dirt we've found."

"Would you mind looking over my notes once I've written them to see if they sound ok?"

Before I could decide whether I would or not, Erica placed her hand on his arm. "There you are, Nick. I've found a cool spot under a tree over there. See the blanket? It will be like a picnic. And I'll be happy to help you with your notes."

She gave me an icy smile. "Gee, Callie, I don't think there's room for you on the blanket, but I'm sure you can find somebody who will eat with you. Maybe that foreign student—he's rather out of place, too, isn't he?"

She dragged Nick away before I could reply. I seethed inside. "Bitch! Who is she to be so patronizing? Out of place!"

I found a large flat stone under a tree that also offered a breeze, and sat by myself. From where I ate, I could see most of the students, including Erica and Nick. She was fawning over him, placing herself so that his eyes couldn't help but look at the gap in her low-cut tank top. For once it didn't infuriate me. What she was doing seemed sad.

And then I began to see Erica with new eyes. I remembered how she grumbled at me when I was near her father, or near Nick. She kept her eyes constantly on Nick, who obviously enjoyed her attention, but also looked at other things around him. When his eyes wandered from her, a spasm of fear crossed her face, and she doubled her efforts to get his attention. All of her efforts appeared seductive, and yet it seemed as if she did it because she was afraid or desperate for love.

I grew uncomfortable at the thought, especially because I sensed the whole idea might apply to me, too. I felt angry at Erica. It was hard to keep feeling generous toward the witch. I glanced over at her father, who was laughing with some students. Where did she have room to complain that she wasn't loved? "You should try my family on for size, sister," I muttered.

We were ordered back to work. As I put my whole weight on the spade to force it into the tough clay, again

64

a feeling came over me of being watched. Maybe it was just more of my imagination. But the weird feeling of exposure never left me, and I could even sense in which direction the watcher lay.

I sighed when Dr. Petersen called an early halt to the excavation, explaining he was giving us a break because it was Friday. I was glad to help gather the tools and load the bus, secretly hoping to hurry away from whoever was hunting me.

When the bus arrived back at the University, I unlocked the bike at the rack and rode home. It was a hot afternoon and I was thoroughly soaked by the time I locked the bike in the garage. I dug the key to the kitchen door out of my pocket, only to find the knob unlocked.

Frankie stood in the kitchen wearing a bikini and white cover shirt, sunglasses on top of her dark hair. "Hi, Callie. Have a nice day? You look hot. Why don't you change into your suit and we can go soak in the pool together?"

The air-conditioning was so refreshing, I almost said no. But I wanted a chance to know her better. "That sounds great."

We took her little Toyota to the University pool, which Frankie predicted would be packed, and it was. We laid our stuff in a corner not likely to be splashed, and jumped in.

"So, you got in awfully late last night. Bart called and said the bus had broken down. How do you like your class?"

"It's interesting. And it's certainly not dull."

She arched an eyebrow, and I explained about the events last night, leaving out the part about the knife. She would probably feel responsible for my safety, and might even insist I drop the course.

She frowned while I talked. "I hope that's not Jon's way of introducing you kids to the Caddo folklore," she said, meaning the chanting and strange voices. "He's been known to do rather—er—creative things in the past."

"What?"

She sighed and hung on to the side of the pool while kicking her feet. "I guess wives always tend to see things from their husband's point of view, and I try to be objective. But Walt has told me some of the stunts Jon's pulled in the department, and it's hard for me to be objective about him. He once dressed as a mummy to remind some of his upper level students that archaeology wasn't all carbon-14 analysis. I mean, it's just not professional. He's a nice guy, don't get me wrong."

She saw that I was having a hard time believing that he could have concocted the situation last night. "Maybe I'm not being fair. He's done a lot of work for the department, and Walt could have been repeating rumors started by jealous staff members."

I nodded vigorously. "He doesn't strike me as the type to use gimmicky tricks at all. He was very concerned about our safety last night. And anyway, it has to be someone else who is harassing him. He wouldn't destroy his own lab."

"You're probably right. It all smacks of a student's prank to me, anyway."

I wanted to change the subject. How could she have such an opposite impression of Dr. Petersen?

"So tell me about yourself. Why did you decide to become a professor of English?"

She laughed. "It does sound a bit boring, doesn't it? But it's never been boring for me. Let's see. From my earliest memories, I always had a love of books. Libraries were some of my favorite haunts. When I came to college, I fell in love with the atmosphere and unique way of life.

"Besides, when I graduated, I felt I had barely scratched the surface of world literature. So I stayed in school until I had my Ph.D."

66

"Have you taught at Weches State since you gradu-ated?"

"No, I first taught at a small college in Illinois. But it was only a three-year assignment and I didn't have tenure. So I came here."

"And that's when you met Dr. Broussard?"

"Eventually, yes. But not at first. We didn't run in the same circles. I went to talk with him when I was writing a paper on Native American folklore. That was a couple of years ago. We've been inseparable since." She ended with the bubbly smile of a newlywed.

I was amused. "So if you're my surrogate mother, tell me about my surrogate father. He seems nice, but he's rather hard to know."

She became more serious. "Well, Callie, he's had a hard life. I think one of the reasons I love him so much is that he has accomplished a lot in his life despite many difficult circumstances."

I nodded. "The other night, he mentioned someone named Melanie. I got the impression she died."

"He said that? I'm surprised. He rarely talks about it, and he must think a great deal of you to have even mentioned that."

"I'm sorry, I didn't mean to pry." I held on to the side of the pool and kicked my legs.

"No. You're not prying. It's a difficult thing for a second wife to deal with the constantly reappearing ghost of the first. You see, they had a very happy marriage and were looking forward to having children. And then she discovered that she was infertile. The doctors couldn't do anything. She became obsessed with the idea of bearing her own child. Apparently, she was part Caddo and began to look into the roots of her ancestors' beliefs in hope of finding a cure. Eventually she sought the advice of an old medicine woman."

I stared at her in amazement, preparing to hear the

name of Manitu Flying Eagle. Frankie was wrapped up in her thoughts and didn't see me.

"Walt had been bitterly disappointed that they couldn't have children, but he was willing to consider adoption. When his wife began to lose her grip on sanity, constantly muttering Caddo chants, it was more than he could stand. He took her to a psychiatrist in Houston. It was the doctor's opinion that she needed extensive, full-time counseling and advised that she be committed to a mental institution until her condition improved. Walt was sick about it and has felt guilty ever since. In the end, he committed her because he sincerely believed it was her only hope. Shortly after she arrived, they found she had hung herself with her bed sheets. She had shown no previous signs of suicidal tendencies."

I was shocked. I didn't know what to say. "I'm sorry. You're right. He has done well."

She laughed bitterly. "Oh, that's not the half of it. His mother was a peculiar old lady who believed that demons would attack her kids if they didn't obey her. I guess she thought that it was the only way to make six kids behave when she was poor and raising them alone. All the rest grew up with a great deal of problems. Walt is the only successful one of the bunch."

She sighed and rolled her eyes to the sky. "And then, as if all that wasn't enough, when he was drafted and sent to Vietnam, he saw his best friend blown up in front of him." She shook her head. "Walt is a unique person. Although he is outgoing, he also has an introspective side, and that has been his saving. He has been able to work through all the terrible emotions he has carried and come out on top. In the long run, it has made him a very strong man, and I respect him for it."

The laughter, squeals and radio music drifted around us, but we ignored it. I studied Frankie's thick, dark hair pulled back at her neck and felt a growing love for her.

And I had a strong desire to know this new husband of hers better. I wanted to know how he had survived all the horrible things that had happened to him. Maybe I could learn how to survive the things that were happening to me.

Eight

Early Saturday morning, I sipped coffee in bed and leafed through the pages of my journal. I hadn't written much since I had been here. Everything I could remember from the first day until Friday came pouring out through my pen. I paused, then wrote about yesterday.

It had been a day full of emotions and of contradictions: an eagle feather—was it Manitu Flying Eagle's way of telling me something? Did the spirits exist like she so firmly believed, or was she a hoax? Erica—was she the bitch she appeared to be? Or should I pity her? Did Dr. Petersen use unprofessional ways of teaching his students, or was he a warm, sincere archaeologist? And Walter Broussard, what in him was so strong that it could overcome so many terrible events, and yet come out a well-balanced human being, successful in his career? "I'd like to know more about Dr. B," I wrote.

A phone rang in another part of the house. Someone knocked at my door. "Come in."

Dr. Broussard stuck his head in. "Wake up, sleepyhead. There's a voice on the phone asking for you, and it sounds like that handsome young Bart you've been seeing. I told your mother I'd have to beat them away from our door."

I blushed. "We're just friends."

He laughed. "So I see. Anyway, I'm going story hounding today. My liquor store friend that Frankie gets such a kick out of has heard of a farmer who claims his family owned that land since white men came to Texas. I'll be gone the better part of the day." He winked at me. "Behave yourself, now."

"Of course." I followed him out to the phone.

"Have a good sleep, Callie?" Bart asked.

"Why does everyone think I sleep late?"

"Oh, then you're ready for me to pick you up now?"

I glanced down at my robe and slippers and ran my hand through my messy hair. "No."

"Ha. Thought as much. I'm working anyway. Just called to see if you'd be interested in a late lunch. I'll be through here around twelve-thirty or one, but I'll have to go home and shower. I can pick you up after that. What do you say?"

"Sounds great. Then what?"

"Oh, we'll think of something," he hinted coyly.

"I think I'd better think of something."

"Hey, Callie, you need to trust me. See you later."

After I dressed, paying particular attention to my hair and make-up, I met Frankie in the hall carrying a broom and dust pan.

"Can I help?" I felt a bit guilty for not doing more around the house.

"Sure, I'd appreciate it. Walt's done his chores this morning, and I've just started mine."

We worked on the house for quite a while before Frankie called a halt. "Let's don't overdo it."

The telephone rang on the hall table I had been dusting. "I'll get it. It's probably Bart saying he's running late. Hello?"

There was no reply on the other end though I could tell it had not been hung up.

"Hello? If you don't answer I'm going to hang up."

A hiss came over the receiver, gradually growing into a chanted whisper. "Wasichu. Wasichu. Death to the Wasichu. Touch our bones and die, trespasser."

"Who is this!" The voice chilled me and I shivered.

"The Caddo animus will show you the right path," the whisper said ominously. "Drink the tea which washes clean, the herb that purifies. Then we will bother you no more. Then you will see the truth and not touch our bones. Drink the tea of the spirit of the Caddoes before it is too late."

The line hissed loudly. Was that some static on the line or him? "The herb has been shown to you. Drink the tea and prevent the death of the Wasichu. Their lives are in your hands. You have been warned." The phone clicked, then gave the dial tone.

I replaced the receiver, then walked directly to my room. With a kick, the door shut behind me and I stood facing the dresser, staring at the top drawer. With a firm resolve, I opened the drawer, dug underneath my polo shirts to the knife that had been thrown at me and pulled it out.

I glanced at the clock: 12:26. Bart should be almost through, but he wouldn't be here for a while. The phone rang again and I jumped. I heard Frankie say, "Just a minute and I'll get her." I shoved the knife into my purse and flopped on the bed.

She rapped on the door. "Telephone."

In the hall, I looked nervously at the receiver a second, then picked it up. Whoever it was could go to hell. "Hello."

"Guess what, Callie? I'm done and showered and ready to pick you up. Just thought I'd give you a call in case you weren't ready."

"Bart, it's you. Sure, I'm ready any time."

"Of course it's me. Who else were you expecting?"

My hand covered my forehead. "I don't know, to tell you the truth."

"Hey, are you all right? You don't sound like yourself."

I sighed. "I had a strange phone call and it shook me up."

"Who was it? What did they say?"

"I'll tell you when you arrive."

When he came through the door, he followed my lead in cheerfully teasing Frankie about her hole-filled shirt and shorts instead of talking about the call. Several times when she wasn't looking he cast a worried glance my way. Frankie pretended to attack us with a broom, and we left. In the truck, we decided on lunch at a hamburger place.

Bart pulled up to a stop sign, looked at me with serious blue eyes. "Ok, I can't stand it any more. Tell me about the phone call."

I let out the breath I had been holding. "It was a threatening whisper—the same voice that we heard in the woods that night. Actually it wasn't me that was threatened. It was more like everyone having anything to do with the excavation was threatened. And the voice said their lives were in my hands."

"Now wait a minute. Either you were threatened or you weren't." He pulled into a parking space at the restaurant and put the truck in park, but left on the air conditioner. "Think carefully about it."

I stared at the bright, cloud-filled sky and concentrated. "He kept saying Wasichu. I got the idea that it was a Caddo slur for whites, something not very nice. He said if we touched their bones, we would die." I paused, trying to remember. "Then he said something about everything would be ok if I drank the tea. Drinking the tea would prevent their deaths. By drinking it, I would see the truth and not touch their bones. Something like that."

Bart's eyes were fixed on me. "That's strange. I wonder what he was talking about. What tea? Have you received a tea bag in the mail?"

73

"Not in the mail, but . . ."

"But what?"

I dug into my purse and produced the knife. My hands shook as I held it out. The eagle feather and dried herb dangled from the handle. We both stared at it for a moment, neither of us touching it.

"You wouldn't be so stupid as to boil those leaves and drink them, would you?"

"No, of course not. Give me a little credit. I might go see a Caddo shaman, but I'm not going to drink an unknown plant."

"You smoked one."

I grimaced. "Yes, that was stupid, though I didn't notice you refusing. Anyway, that turned out ok, and I can learn from my mistakes. Besides, she didn't throw it at me on a knife."

"You have a point, but we both need to be more careful, especially you. So what do you plan to do with it?"

"I'll know after we hit the campus library."

"The library? Why?"

"Because somewhere in that library is a book with a picture and description of this weed, and we're going to find it."

By silent agreement, we decided not to speak about it while we were in the restaurant. The conversation, between bites of burgers, was mainly about family.

"So how has Erica been at the site? You haven't mentioned her."

I rolled my eyes. "She's been ok, I guess."

"What does that mean?"

I told him about how possessively she acted around Nick and her father, and that it was hard for me to understand.

"Oh, that's easy. She's jealous of you. You're very pretty, you know."

I looked down to cover the blush and could feel him watching me closely. I'd never thought of myself as pretty. As a distraction, I grabbed my cola and drank. "You know, I began to wonder if she was jealous about something. But why your dad and Nick? I'm not on the make for either of them. Rather than be angry at her, I feel sorry that that's the only way she knows how to act. It's pitiful that she can only flirt with guys, and not become friends with them."

He smiled, and his blue eyes glistened. "You're sharp."

His hand covered mine, which was resting on the table. I knew any other girl would have killed for an opportunity like this with Bart. But I only felt uncomfortable, without knowing exactly why.

Trying not to be obvious about it, I slipped my hand away and used both hands to finish my hamburger.

In less than an hour, we were in the University library. At the information desk, a student was reading a textbook and marking certain spots with a highlighting pen. She glanced at us with bored eyes. "May I help you?"

I stepped forward. "I found a plant and I don't know what it is. Where would I find a book to identify it?"

"Have you tried the professors over at Botany?"

I shook my head. "I want to do this on my own." I didn't want questions about where I got the plant.

"You might try botanical reference books for this region. They would be in the catalogue. And any herbal books are likely to have a lot of pictures of plants which have any uses. Those would also be in the catalogue."

"Thanks."

At the file drawers, I found several possibilities under regional botanical reference, all of which looked quite a bit more technical than what I had in mind. And there were several books under Herbs, Therapeutic Uses. I jotted the call numbers down and headed for the elevators.

We found the 600s behind the bank of elevators on the third floor. The botanicals looked too complicated to be any help. We went down a few more aisles, covered from floor to the top of the eight-foot-high bookcases with thick technical volumes. At last, we found the herbals. We each took a couple and walked to an empty table in a private corner.

"Get out the plant," Bart whispered.

I had separated the plant from the rest of the knife in the truck and had wrapped it in some newspaper. I unfolded it now, leaving it in the open between us.

Most of the descriptions, listed in alphabetical order, used scientific terms. The book I was reading defined each term. It was pointless to try to learn the difference between an oblate and cordate leaf.

My plant had dried blue flowers on top, a hairy stalk and palm-like leaves. Armed with this, I carefully searched through all the pictures and descriptions. I was only half-way through my first book when Bart slammed his book closed.

"This is ridiculous. We ought to go see someone in Botany. They'd probably know it right away."

"We'll do that if we can't find anything here. But if we ask someone, they'll want to know where we got the plant. And they'll probably know who you are. They might talk to your father about it. Depending on what we find, we may not want your father to know."

His shoulders relaxed. "Ok. We can keep at it for a little while longer. And then I have another idea."

"Fine," I said. I flipped passed Leak, Lettuce, and Licorice. Not them. Mint, Mistletoe (which was poisonous, but didn't look like my plant), and Monarda.

On the next page was Monkshood. I stared at the picture, and then down to the description. I went back to the picture, then compared it to the shriveled plant next to the book.

"I think I found it," I said softly. "What do you think?"

He compared the two. "I think you're right. Look at this." He pointed to the word "caution" in bold print.

76

I read in a whisper. " 'Monkshood is among the most poisonous of plants. Small doses can cause painful death in a few hours.' " I whistled softly. Fear seeped into my chest. "So that's what the voice meant by 'the herb that purifies.' Of course they wouldn't bother me any more after I drank it. Because I wouldn't be around to bother them."

"Why would someone want to kill you, Callie?"

The impact of his words hit me deep inside. Suddenly, I felt terribly frightened. "I don't know. Unless I have something, or am about to discover the truth about something that someone else doesn't want known."

"Like what?" His brow wrinkled in worry.

I shrugged.

Bart stood up. "We're not going to wait around for the next attack on your life. We're going straight to the source." He clenched and unclenched his fists.

"What do you mean?" I worried about his fierce reaction, but followed him to the elevator. As I walked, I folded the monkshood back into the newspaper.

"We're going to confront those Caddoes and tell them enough is enough. So they have a gripe against the white man for digging up their ancestors. There are legal ways to handle that, and they could probably win. There's no need to do something like this. And knowing the type of person who would pull this sort of prank, they'll back off when confronted. That's what we're going to do."

When the elevator opened onto the lobby, I had to hurry to keep up with him.

"Wait, Bart. This is crazy. They could be dangerous. And you don't know that they did this."

He glanced over his shoulder. "I'll understand if you don't want to go, Callie. As a matter of fact, it might be safer for you not to."

"Calm down. You're overreacting. You're not going alone. And anyway, I've got the evidence."

77

I ran alongside of him on the way to the truck. He didn't say a word. He backed out with a squeal, and headed for the highway.

He was fuming. "I've had it. They've been threatening Dad all semester. They tore up his lab and scared his class. And now they try to kill you."

I was frightened for him, for us. I had to calm him down. "So how do you know where they are?"

"I passed their camp on the way back to you guys the other night. I pretended to pull in and turn around, but I saw a few of them. They had several tents pitched, and a pickup with Oklahoma license plates and a sticker reading Anadarko Reservation."

"How do you know that it was these Indians who did all these things? Are you completely sure?"

He seemed to lose his resolve. "Sure I'm sure. I mean, it had to be them. Who else would have wanted to?"

"But you don't have any evidence. Isn't that a bit like guilty until proven innocent?"

He glared at me. "How come you're sticking up for them all of a sudden?"

"I'm not sticking up for them. I just don't know for a fact it was them. And I remember the leader being nice. What are you going to do, rush in there and take on six or eight guys in one big fight? You've been seeing too many cowboy movies."

I could tell he was a little insulted by what I was saying, but he became calmer. "All right. So I won't go in slugging. But don't you even want to talk to them about the poison?"

"No, I didn't say that. I'd like their reaction to it." I watched the pine trees roll by. "You know, it's just too neat, like a movie. The Caddoes are the obvious suspects, but this thing with the monkshood was sneaky, underhanded. Someone who is sneaky is smart. And I think a smart person would realize whether or not they would be a suspect before committing murder." Even as

78

I said it, the last word shocked me. Once again, I felt myself being sucked into a dangerous whirlpool that was likely to pull me under.

"You've got a point there. I guess I hadn't really thought this thing through." He lifted his hands briefly from the steering wheel in a shrug. "So why are we going to see the Caddoes?"

"Maybe they can help us."

Bart turned the truck off the road onto a National Forest Campground. He drove to the spot he had seen two evenings ago.

It was empty. Now Bart's suspicions began to grow in me. A great anger kindled deep inside me against whoever threatened my life. I wanted some answers.

Nine

Bart pulled the truck into the parking space by the tent pad and picnic table. We both got out and he walked to the pad, kicked the dirt and swore.

"I knew I should have come back sooner. I was afraid they would sneak away."

I shrugged. "At least this proves one thing. They couldn't have been the ones to make the call today."

"This doesn't prove anything except that they've moved. They could still be around. Or they could be on their way back to the reservation. They could have stopped and given you a call before they left town."

But I had a gut feeling that the Caddoes hadn't done it. "I don't think so."

"What makes you so sure? You believe that just because they are Indian that they are noble or pure?"

"That's not it at all. It's just that I talked briefly with their leader the day of the protest, and he struck me as the type of guy who would do things other people wouldn't like, but he would be honest about having done them. He didn't seem sneaky. I think he'd have the courage to do things openly."

Kicking up a cloud of red dust as it came, a park ranger's jeep bounced down the rutted road and pulled in behind Bart's truck, blocking it.

80

"How y'all doin'?" He put on his cap as he stepped out. He was middle-aged and of average height. His flushed red cheeks contrasted with his dark, rather oily hair. His large beer belly strained against the buttons on his uniform shirt creating such large gaps between the fabric that I wondered how he had buttoned them in the first place.

"Just fine, thanks," I said.

"Good, that's good. Maybe y'all didn't notice the sign when you come in, but this is a fee area. Buck fifty for picnicin'; three bucks for a tent site. Y'all plan on stayin'?"

Bart had joined me by now. "No, sir," he said. "We were just looking for some people that we thought would be here, but they're gone."

I chimed in. "Maybe you saw them? There were several Caddo Indians from the Oklahoma reservation. They had a couple of tents, right, Bart?" Bart nodded.

"Oh, sure. Those folks. They didn't understand we have rules and regulations here. One tent per pad. One feller got real argumentative, sayin' this was Injun land and they shouldn't have to pay, and they otta be able to pitch their tents anywheres they like. Almost had to kick them out. But another guy spoke up and told him to hush. Asked if they was any sites with the tent pads close together and near the lake, so they could fish. You'll find 'em on Loblolly Loop. Y'all aren't plannin' to camp with 'em, are ya? We got a limit of four persons a site."

"No, sir," Bart said. "We just wanted to talk with them before they left."

The ranger took off his hat and mopped his forehead with his sleeve. "They paid through Sunday. Said they most likely leavin' then. If y'all change your mind, you can leave the money in the box by the front gate. Or I'll be around again later and can pick it up then." He climbed back in the jeep, started the engine, and waved.

As he aimed his squeaking chassis down the road, I climbed back into the truck. "So do you know where Loblolly Loop is?"

"We'll find it. This place isn't that big."

Within ten minutes of weaving through the pine-shaded asphalt road, we had found them. Two guys and one girl, all slightly older than us, were at the site; the others were nowhere to be seen. One guy was sitting with his back against a tree facing the lake and didn't turn our way as we got out. The other, with black shoulder-length hair, denim shirt and jeans, stared at us with hostile eyes but didn't speak. The girl observed us briefly with blank eyes, then continued whittling a stick.

"Hi," I said as pleasantly as possible. No response from Hostile Eyes. "We want to talk to you."

Silence.

I tried again. Although I remembered the leader to be honest, I had my doubts about this guy. I decided to be cautiously friendly. "I was at the protest last week. Mind if we sit down?"

No response.

"Stop beating around the bush, Callie," Bart said angrily. "We need to get to the point. Somebody's been threatening my dad's life if he doesn't stop the excavation of that Caddo mound. I want to know who's doing it." He and Hostile Eyes glared at each other for a long moment.

Hostile Eyes finally spoke. "We don't threaten, Wasichu, we act. We aren't cowardly like the lying white man, who thinks nothing of making and breaking promises in one breath."

That word again: Wasichu. I shivered, then watched the guy closely.

Bart took a step forward, his arms straight down at his sides and his hands in fists. "His lab has been wrecked, his life threatened, and now Callie," he tilted his head

82

toward me, "has had an attack on her life. She doesn't have anything to do with it, except that she happened to enroll in his class. She's innocent." His voice grew louder. "And yet a knife is thrown at her, and she's encouraged to drink a tea that turns out to be a deadly poison!"

The young Indian was equally angry and also took a step forward, his fists clinched and resting on his hips. "The white man thinks nothing of murdering innocent thousands and you come to us complaining of one person's life who is alive and healthy? More lies and accusations! Your laws say we are innocent until you show we aren't, yet your mind says guilty."

I could see Bart was about to spit out a hot reply, when the young man from behind the tree said firmly, "Enough, John." He arose and walked to Hostile Eyes John, putting a hand on his shoulder and squeezing it as if to help relieve the other's tension. "This is no way to greet guests. My name is Sam Running Wolf."

He stuck out his hand first to me. He was the leader at the protest. He stared deep into my eyes, and I met his gaze squarely. He was as honest as I remembered. I was going to have to start trusting my instincts. I took his hand. "I'm Callie Davis, and this is Bart Petersen."

He held my hand a moment longer, squeezed it, then offered it to Bart. Bart glared at the outstretched hand, and then reluctantly took it.

Sam smiled broadly and indicated his friend. "John here is a bit touchy about being accused of things just because he's an Indian." It sounded like an apology on the surface, but it had its intended effect.

Bart colored. "I'm sorry. I shouldn't have come at you like that, John. You're right. I was ready to hang you before the jury came in. It's just that two of the people I really care about have been threatened, and it makes me jumpy. No hard feelings?" He stuck out a hand to John.

83

My mind was whirling with Bart's change of attitude. The fact that he included me as one of the people he cared for didn't clear my thinking.

Sam maintained the smile on his lips but his eyes were serious as he continued watching Bart. "He's made a sincere apology. Let's shake on it, ok, John?"

John glowered at Bart's hand as if he would spit on it, then grabbed it briefly and stalked off.

"There, now," Sam said evenly. "Now we can begin again. What do you say we all have a seat?"

As Bart seemed tongue-tied, I told Sam about all the threatening events. Throughout the story, his dark brown eyes never left the dirt in front of him nor showed any expression. When I told him about the phone call this morning and the results of the library search, he asked to see the plant. I dug in my purse for the bundle, unwrapped the paper and laid it before him. He agreed that it was monkshood.

"It's not native to this region. It grows mainly in the mountains."

I was puzzled. "So where would someone get this? It was fresh when it was thrown at me that night."

He arched one eyebrow. "Oh, there are several mail order catalogues that carry herbs. It's possible that someone grew this in a flower garden, or maybe they knew it was poisonous. Either way, it would be easy to grow. You say the voice encouraged you to make a tea of this? There's enough here to kill you, yes."

I sighed as I studied the now dry leaves and stem in the wrinkles of newspaper, scattered about the knife blade and handle. The feather was bent on one end. A thought occurred to me. "Say, do you know Manitu Flying Eagle? She's a Caddo shaman who lives around here."

He shook his head. "I don't know of any Caddo shamans in this part of the country."

"That's funny. I would have thought you would know her. She's incredible. Bart and I went to see her. She

84

seemed to know all about me. Using some Native American tarot cards, she told me I was in danger and that others were, too. She said that it was up to me to find my enemy before it was too late."

His eyes narrowed. "That doesn't sound like a Caddo shaman."

I shrugged. "Well, she's proved right so far. And because she warned me, I was watching for trouble and managed to miss the knife and be suspicious of the tea."

He frowned. "That isn't our way. We seek the spirits individually. A shaman is mainly one who knows herbs and healing. A Caddo would not use those cards. They are not from the Earth Peoples."

I started to protest again, but then his words sunk in. I stared at the monkshood. Bart whistled.

Sam spoke softly. "I don't know who's trying to kill you, but you must not trust anyone, not even me. If it's any comfort to you, we are the obvious attackers. I wouldn't think a smart killer would make himself obvious, and this guy sounds smart. We have the simplest motive. But we wouldn't kill to stop this dig. We are not like the white man."

My face must have reflected my confusion and fear. "At the protest, you told me that you weren't finished yet, that we would hear from you."

He nodded, and I could see that he was sympathetic. "And you will. There is a front page article coming out in tomorrow's *Weches Dispatch* telling our side. We'll leave tomorrow as soon as we have a copy. But when we're home, we'll contact the American Civil Liberties Union to pursue it through the U.S. courts. As I said, we're not finished. We won't make it easy for people to violate our burial grounds."

I felt embarrassed that I was one of those digging up his ancestors. I wanted to explain about it being a salvage project, but I didn't want an argument with him. None of us spoke for a while.

At last, Bart stood and offered his hand. "Good luck. I know my dad's work puts us on opposite sides, but that doesn't mean I can't sympathize with you."

Sam and I rose, and he took Bart's hand. "I hope you find your madman before someone is hurt."

As we drove away, I wondered at Sam Running Wolf's last words. He had called our enemy a madman. Why?

I froze. I recalled Frankie's words about how Dr. Petersen would occasionally pull weird pranks as a method of teaching his students.

I glanced at Bart out of the corner of my eye. Could his father be buckling under too much pressure? Could he be sabotaging his own excavation as a means of punishing himself for something? I forced my eyes back onto the road. I couldn't tell Bart about this. I'd just have to keep an eye on Dr. Petersen myself. If he was behind all this, he was bound to slip up some time.

As the days in the field went by, the excavation progressed steadily. Everyone seemed to be doing well, and the deeper into the surface we dug, the more the underlying excitement built. We all wondered who would be the first to find an artifact.

I should say that everyone was doing well but me. The balks between each square became more sharply defined. In each square, the layers of dirt changed color, texture, or type every few inches. That is, everyone's balks but mine.

Maybe I wasn't digging right. Maybe I had mixed the soil leaving a jumbled mess for walls. Dale, Karen, and even Dr. Petersen came to inspect my work from time to time. Each rather impatiently explained the techniques to me and wanted to know if I was sure that I was following their instructions. I assured them I was. But the more they questioned me, the more I wondered if maybe this course was too hard for me after all. Once, I saw the three of them talking quietly together with several glances in my direction, and Dr. Petersen shook his head sadly back and forth. I turned my back so I wouldn't have to watch them.

I knew they were watching me. What's more, I felt someone else watching, too. I tried to ignore it, but I had always found it difficult to ignore the stares of a stranger in a crowd; I always had to look. And so I searched the trees, but could see nothing. For some reason, I kept scanning the top of the tree line as if a person had climbed into the crowns of the loblolly pines to hide from me. One day, I noticed something beyond the trees. Karen said it was a Forest Service fire tower and would no doubt be manned from time to time during the summer and fall when the chance of fires increased.

I tried to avoid staring at it, but couldn't help but pass an eye in that direction occasionally.

The truly odd thing about my square was that the other students working on the mound did not have the same results. In some ways, I expected to find disturbed layers of dirt since this was, after all, a burial mound. If you dig a hole for a body naturally one layer of dirt would mix with another after you shoveled it back. But the mound had been built more than a thousand years ago. The land had changed a lot since then. Old layers had worn away and new dirt deposited. Even so, my area didn't look like any of the other squares at all.

For one thing, there were more river-rounded rocks in my square. That meant the shoveling went slower. It also meant that I spent a lot more time screening smaller amounts of dirt, even though I picked out the larger stones. I couldn't really say I was digging through "layers." It all seemed to be one big mess.

Before long, one guy who was excavating a house found the first artifact: a pottery shard. Everyone stopped what they were doing to peer around shoulders for a glance at it. We all felt as if we had just found a priceless object—which it was—and that we all had a claim on it. Dr. Petersen identified it immediately as typical of the Caddoes at the time the site was built. He was flushed with enthusiasm as he handed it to Dale and Karen, and then back to the proud student, who promptly put it in a specimen bag and made a show out of making notes. The rest of us envied him and went back to our squares inspired.

At the break, Dr. Petersen lectured on pottery making and design. Through his eyes, we began to see that this shard had been part of a vessel. That vessel had been made by a woman and had served a useful life with her. The woman had been born to parents, grew into womanhood, and probably raised children and maybe grandchildren. There had been many people alive at the time the pot had been made, and each had a complete life and a different personality, just like all of us were different. That was what we were trying to understand, at least as much as possible.

Other students turned up flint scrapers, chips, axes, and whole and broken arrowheads and spear points. One found what was apparently a potter's refuse heap with hundreds of potsherds. Dr. Petersen was delighted, sure that once the pieces were back in the lab, that they would yield several whole or nearly whole pots.

I looked with envy on the happy, busy people around me. Even Erica had a first: She discovered the first campfire site, complete with charcoal remains. Her father congratulated her, saying he would use some of the charcoal for tree ring dating. She proudly turned her mocking eyes on me as he made the announcement.

The students working on the mound uncovered bones in their areas. One of the Three (Dr. Petersen, Karen, or Dale) was always close to supervise this stage, hoping to prevent unnecessary damage to the remains. For the most part, their help was not needed, because the bones were so old they had already either crumbled, making it tedious to remove each fleck and place it in a bag, or mineralized from the iron-rich soil, giving them added strength and an orangish color.

My only saving grace at this point was that I was not nearly as deep as they were, as I was still picking out stream rocks. Dr. Petersen speculated that my side of the mound might have been washed away by a stream long ago, and then when the course changed, the stones were deposited. I was depressed. Besides a geology lesson, the only thing I was getting was a good tan.

One evening shortly after the third set of human bones was found, we all decided to work late. The day had been low in humidity, a rarity during the East Texas summers. By now, we had learned that despite the heat, the work had dramatically increased our appetites, so we always brought plenty of food, and had even brought dishes to share. Lunch time became like a picnic. Today there had been way too much food, which meant we had enough for a supper at the site.

We sat underneath the trees at dusk, feeling a little of what it must have felt for the Caddoes to come in from a long day in the fields. Since one of the Three now drove the bus, parking it at the site so that we didn't need a bus driver, we knew we could take our time and leave when we wanted to. We had developed a sense of fellowship and enjoyed singing around a fire, always built in a remote area to avoid adding to the evening's heat. As time wore on, some of the students, who brought their own cars so they wouldn't be stranded, decided to head back to the dorms.

We were packing up when we heard the chanting again, this time growing more quickly to a loud, raspy whisper. Some students, who had not been with the rest of us the first time, were not sure what it was. Dr. Petersen shouted into the woods. "Who the hell are you and what do you want? Make your point, then beat it."

The chanting stopped, and a whispering voice began in its place, at first indecipherable, then all too clear. "Wasichu. Wasichu. Death to the Wasichu. You have disturbed our bones, violated our holy ground. Now you will pay the consequences. Death to the Wasichu."

I knew the voice. It was the same one I had heard making the threat to me.

"I think it's time for us to get out of here," one guy said.

Karen and Dale flashed powerful beams of light through the forest. There was some movement. Both beams centered on it. From behind a bush stepped Nick and Erica, who was fumbling with a button on her blouse. Both acted embarrassed. Dr. Petersen grew furious, which stopped the few chuckles from the class.

"I think you two have some explaining to do," he said, and I realized the mysterious voice had stopped.

"It's not like you think, sir," Nick said, fear creeping into his voice.

Erica flashed her ready smile. "Daddy, we were just getting some more fire wood when we heard the voice starting. And you'll never guess what happened. We saw someone in the forest. We tried to creep up on him, but he ran away at the last minute. Aren't you proud of us!"

Ten

The next day at the site, Erica had lost her spunk. She worked quietly, her face appearing worn out or sad, and her eyes always in her square. No doubt she and her father had had words, because the two avoided contact with each other all day. Only Karen or Dale stopped to review her progress or Nick's.

My own square continued to be a frustration. Out of laziness, I had not put anything into my field notebook for two days, and now needed to catch up, so dug through my pack looking for the notebook. A summer that had begun by looking interesting sure seemed to have a roadblock at every turn.

It wasn't there. I quickly checked all the pockets again. "I've lost my field notebook," I said to Karen as she passed by the shady trees where I stood. I shook all the contents onto the cool grass at my feet.

"Have you checked your square? Perhaps it's there."

"Good idea." I moved out of the shade of the pine and flipped my sunglasses down from my head as the light seared my eyes. I checked the square and even under loose dirt around it. I looked in the squares next to mine. No notebook.

"I still can't find it," I told Karen with my hands on my hips. I became frantic. All of my lecture notes, the

91

general site records, measurements and sketches, as well as the detailed notes and drawings of my own square were in it. Much of it was irreplaceable.

Karen put her own notebook down and stood to join me. She put a hand on my shoulder to calm me. "We'll find it. It can't be far. Perhaps it slipped from the pouch to the floor of the bus this morning. Let's check."

We climbed into the bus. My heart fell as we searched under the seats. Somehow, I knew it wouldn't be there. When Karen left to talk to another student, I stood on the steps looking over the site and the students scattered underneath trees. "What can I do? I might be able to copy the notes from someone else, but nobody did my measuring for me. And there is no way to replace the notes on my square."

I felt sick. I vaguely heard Dr. Petersen call everyone back to work. I stared at them as they slowly came to their feet. I remembered Dr. Petersen's glowing confidence in me the first day we had talked. He was so pleased that I was interested in his life's work at such a young age. And now, not only was my square unfruitful, but I had lost my notes as well.

When I realized that this might be the first grade on my college transcript, I felt worse. All the companies I would send it to would see this grade before all others. "How does it feel to begin college by failing, Callie, old girl?" I muttered.

I was about to step off the bus when I caught a glimpse of Erica. Her eyes held mine for less than a second and turned away. But I could have sworn she smirked at me.

I thought about running to Karen and saying, "Erica's taken my notebook and I'm going to get it now. She's really done it this time, the bitch."

But something held me back. "Wait," I told myself. "Don't do things without thinking. Think of why she stole the notebook. You must have proof to accuse people."

I thought back. I could still see the look on her face after she saw I was hunting for it. She was smiling as if she enjoyed my misery. But Erica wasn't being smart when she did it, if she did it. After all, now Karen knew about the missing notebook and would look out for something that seemed copied.

If Erica copied from it, that is. She could have simply taken it for spite and thrown it away. "If you want your notebook, you're going to have to be smarter than she is." In my mind I heard a phrase that Grandmother used to say: "You catch more flies with honey than vinegar. That means you must use your heart."

Then I began to argue with myself, which they say is always a bad sign. "Right. I should walk over to her and say, 'Gee, I'm glad you took my notebook, Erica.' That's crazy. I hate her."

But as I looked out at Erica, I saw her staring at two girls who worked close together and who were laughing and joking with each other. Erica looked longingly at them, and then her face turned sad. I knew then. She acted hateful to me because for some reason she was jealous, maybe of the way I seemed to make friends so quickly. Maybe in her own way she was crying for a friend. Then I remembered another of my grandmother's sayings. "It is a wise woman who can make her enemies into her friends."

I certainly didn't want to become like Erica: bitter, without friends, lonely. Lonely. I had been lonely during the last year. I knew what loneliness was. And both of us had helped to bring it on ourselves.

I sighed. "So what should I do? I need my notebook back."

Then the answer came to me clear and strong. "Trust your instincts. Use honey."

I went back to my square to begin digging again. All afternoon, I couldn't keep my mind on my work. It didn't take much concentration anyway, since I hadn't

93

uncovered even a small pottery fragment or stone flake. I watched Erica out of the corner of my eye, being careful not to let her know that I saw her glances in my direction. I worked at looking busy, but watched for an opportunity to confront her. I didn't know what I would say, but I knew what I had to do.

At last I saw her take a load of dirt to the main sifter. No one else was around. I walked over with some dirt in a box, set it down, and helped her sift hers.

She glanced at me, confused. I pretended to be pleasantly satisfied with the day.

She spoke first in her normal sugary/back-stabbing voice. "So how's your square coming? Found anything yet?"

I gulped back a sarcastic reply. Everyone knew the trouble I was having. I put on the sincerest smile I could manage. "No, nothing yet. But I keep trying. Eventually something will turn up, or maybe I'll dig through to China. They have a lot of artifacts there. I'd be coming at them from underneath; that would be an archaeological first." The thought genuinely amused me.

She forced a laugh. "Sure. A first." She looked uncomfortable and went back to sifting. I quietly continued to help her. She spoke again. "So, are you going to be ready for the midterm checks?" She meant the midterm notebook grading. Because our notes were so important to the course, they were to count as half our grade.

I pretended to think. "I believe so. I've let a friend borrow it to catch up on the field notes." Then I snapped my fingers. "Darn."

She looked puzzled as she pushed back a strand of blond hair. "What's wrong?"

"Oh, I forgot to put some important things in there, so the notes aren't complete. I guess I'll need to ask for it back for a little while, so my friend can have all the information."

She pursed her carefully sculpted eyebrows. "You mean you're letting someone have all your notes? Can't you get into trouble? And that would mean you were letting your, uh, friend, have the advantage of all your work."

I looked directly in her eyes. "Yes, all that's true. But real friendship is something you can't put a price on. It's rare and precious. So who cares about a few notes?" I smiled again and turned to go.

She called to me. "Hey, Callie. You didn't sift your dirt."

I spoke over my shoulder. "That's ok. There's nothing in it anyway."

As I stood on my balk, I smiled, more pleased with myself than I could ever remember. I knew I had done something good, something kind. I jumped onto the dirt floor of my square, looking at the work I had done.

Somehow, a grade didn't seem all that important now. I wondered at the change that had taken place inside of me: so simple, such a short conversation, and yet such a different feeling inside. I felt proud that I had trusted myself. I watched Erica, and found that I no longer hated her. I pitied her. I didn't want to spend my life acting in the desperate ways she did. How lonely it must be to not love yourself or to think yourself loved.

I thought about my notebook and shrugged. Now it didn't upset me that it might not be returned. I could redo probably more of it than I first thought, anyway. It just didn't seem to matter compared to what I felt inside me.

Later that evening, when we took our seats on the bus, I was only mildly surprised to see the notebook laying in my usual place. I saw there was a note inside it. I took a seat, and saw Karen silently slide into the bench behind me, nodding at the book in my hands.

The note read: "Dear Callie. Your friend gave me this to return to you, saying that she didn't copy out of it, but appreciated your offer. She said she thought that true friends wouldn't use each other's school work. She said she was glad that you considered her a friend. Erica."

I felt someone's eyes on me, and saw that Erica was watching for my reaction. I smiled at her.

She slowly smiled a little, then looked down as if ashamed. She turned to face the front.

When we arrived back at the bus stop on campus, Dr. Petersen motioned Erica to his car and they left before the rest of us had unloaded.

As I mounted Frankie's bike and rode for a short distance on the sidewalk, the chain slipped off its sprocket and I cursed. It had been a long day, and I was tired. I leaned it against some tall shrubs and sat down on grass to fix it. I could see that the chain was too loose and would need to be tightened.

While I removed the tools from the pack underneath the seat, I heard voices from behind the shrub and recognized them as Dale and Karen's as they walked down the sidewalks.

"I think you're trying to read too much into it," Dale said.

Karen snorted. "You're just not observant. Haven't you seen how jumpy he's getting? I've watched him open his mail with dread, only to be relieved when nothing unusual is in it. And he watches the woods out at the site as if he were hoping to have a glimpse of the prankster. I tell you, he's becoming paranoid."

"Well, who wouldn't be if you had received the number of threats as he has? Anyway, nothing serious has happened and I'll bet he thinks there won't be any more incidents."

"Nothing serious has happened? What about that knife thrown at Callie Davis? And you might recall that the lab was torn up."

"Ok. So why didn't Dr. Petersen have the University Police come to the site? Then everyone could feel safer."

"You know that there would be articles in the paper about it, and we received enough heat from that piece interviewing those Caddo yahoos. Parents would complain that it's unsafe to continue the excavation, and the University would shut us down."

Dale's voice grew fainter as they walked down the path. "I guess you're right. But I don't see any signs that he's cracking under the strain. What makes you think . . ."

I strained to hear Karen's reply. "It was the way he lashed out at Dr. Broussard, blaming him for all this. If that isn't strange, I don't know what is." At last, they were too far away for me to hear.

The chain was back on the sprocket, and on an impulse, I headed for the house where Bart and a couple of his friends were replacing shingles. I remembered my fears that Dr. Petersen might be trying to wreck the project as a punishment to himself. "It's time Bart and I talked about it." I turned onto one of the main side streets leading away from the campus.

Bart was stacking some remaining bundles of shingles neatly against the house for tomorrow and waving goodbye to his coworkers, who were driving off in a blue Chevy.

"Hi, Cal. I didn't expect to see you today." He gathered up tools and took them to the tool box on the back of his truck. He untied his nail apron and placed it in there, too. "What's up?"

I hesitated. "I need to talk to you about something but I don't know how to start."

"Sounds serious. Listen, I'm hot and thirsty. Why don't we go some place for a cold drink. Then we can talk." Sweat had soaked his t-shirt and shorts.

I nodded. He knocked on the front door of the house, removing his cap. A gray-haired woman appeared, and he told her he was going for the day. He explained the problems with her roof which he had found, and that he expected to be through tomorrow. Meanwhile, I loaded the bike into the bed of the truck and climbed in the hot cab.

He opened the door, pulled off his shirt and took a fresh one off the seat. Despite the perspiration, I couldn't help but notice his muscular chest.

At a local sandwich shop, we chose a booth away from the large speakers booming rock music. "So what's up?" he asked after the waiter had taken our orders.

"It's about your dad."

He nodded as he pulled a comb through his damp hair. "He mentioned last night that there had been another attempt to frighten the students away."

"That's right. And he was very angry about it. How is he acting at home?"

"Why?"

"I told you at the beginning of this course that I would keep an eye on him for you. You said you would share any information you had with me so we could both figure out what is happening."

He didn't look satisfied with my answer. "All right. He seems to be more grouchy than usual. He and I have hardly spent any time together, but that's not unusual during his summer field classes. And he seems very angry with Erica, which is not unusual."

"I guess he didn't tell you. When the voices began in the woods, Erica and Nick were caught making out. When they came back into the clearing, their clothes looked rumpled and dirty."

Bart whistled. "I guess that would piss him off."

I brushed this aside. "Anything else?"

"I don't think so. What are you driving at?"

The waiter brought our drinks and I played with my straw. I didn't know how to say it without insulting him, so I just plunged in. "Remember when we saw the Caddoes and Sam said to be suspicious of everyone? I thought it was good advice, so I decided to watch

98

everyone who had anything to do with the site, including your dad. So I began to wonder, if he was behind all these ghostly appearances, what would be his motive?"

"Now wait a minute," Bart said hotly.

"Hear me out. So I thought, what if he were feeling badly about something he had done or thought he had done, and wanted to punish himself for it?"

Bart sighed and rolled his eyes. "Callie, my dad and I have been having heart-to-heart talks all my life. He has told me things that he wouldn't tell Mom. I understand what you're saying, but believe me, he's just not the type. It's not that I'm being defensive, though I suppose I am. But he seems to have a very healthy way of dealing with guilt. He believes your mistakes are an opportunity to learn something and that there's no use getting depressed about something that you can't change. He thinks you have to pick yourself up and do the best you can the next time around. What started you thinking about this?"

I told him Karen's speculation that his dad was under too much pressure, and how he had angrily accused Dr. Broussard for being responsible for all the weird events.

Bart sipped his drink. "I don't know what to think of that. But I do know that there have been some bad feelings between Dr. Broussard and Dad for several years, though Dad hasn't talked much about it. If he accused Dr. Broussard of anything, maybe he was just frustrated and angry about the hassles he's been having. And another thing, he's not the sort of person who shifts blame away from himself onto other people. He owns up to what he's done."

"Ok. I'm convinced. Sorry. I just wanted to see how you felt about it."

He was calmer now and winked at me. "No problem. Now I can take you home."

As he drove into the driveway, he put the truck in park but didn't turn off the engine. He slid across the bench seat toward me with an unmistakable intention. He leaned over and kissed me softly, wanting to make it a lingering caress, but I cut it short. My heart was pounding. My mind shouted, "What is wrong with me? Why don't I want him to touch me?"

He began another kiss, and on impulse, I made it a loud, fake smack. "Ah, my love," I said, pretending to be serious, "I regret that I can continue this no more, because, behold, you stinketh!"

He threw his head back and laughed. "I stink? Take a whiff of your underarms, lady! You haven't been inside all day drinking lemonade."

I reached for the door handle and opened it. "Then we must say adieu. Until tomorrow!" I theatrically waved farewell, pulled my bike out of the back, and headed to the door. As I entered, I let out my breath, relieved that I had survived another uncomfortable situation with him.

Totally confused with myself and my motives, I headed for the bathroom and a long, cold shower.

Eleven

I sat on my bed, trying to force the comb through a knot at the end of my kinky dark hair. As I pulled at the tangle, I thought how silly it was to keep it long during such a hot summer, and resolved to at least put it up off my shoulders when I went out to the site. I finished, cleaned the hair from my brush and put it in the trash basket. I pulled my journal from under the bed and wrote about the day's emotional ups and downs. I wrote about being a butterfly flying in a high wind, now making excellent progress, now whirled around and flung at obstacles.

I heard Frankie lightly knock and enter. I motioned her to the opposite twin bed and continued jotting down the current line in my head.

"What's new," I said, putting my pen down.

She made a show of being modest, but I could tell she was excited about something. "Oh, nothing much, really."

"Come on, Frankie. Out with it."

She gave me a sly grin. "Oh, it can wait. How was your day?"

"I'll tell you about it after I hear your news. Something good has happened, hasn't it?"

She didn't need any further encouragement. "Well, perhaps I'm not the most brilliant English professor who ever lived, but I have had a paper accepted for publication." When she named the journal, even I had heard of it and was impressed.

"Congratulations."

She gushed how much it meant to her and how it was bound to impress the other professors in the department. "You know what this will mean? I think I'll finally be assigned a graduate course to teach." Apparently teaching graduate students was a prize handed out only to a few.

In her enthusiasm, she discussed her various departmental rivals and how they would react to the article. At last her excitement waned, and she resumed her interest in me. "So tell me about your day. I've certainly bored you long enough with mine."

"It wasn't as eventful as yours, but I did do something I'm proud of." Slowly at first because I was watching for her reaction, and then more quickly, I told her about the episode with Erica, how my feelings changed toward her, then how I confronted her. By this time, Frankie was smiling proudly at me. When I told her the part about the notebook on the bus seat and Erica's note inside, she reached across and hugged me.

"I'm proud of you, Callie. Very few adults would have done as well in that situation. I bet you feel good about yourself. And you trusted your instincts. Very good."

I blushed and nodded. "I didn't even care if the notebook was returned or not. That was the up side of my day. There was also a down side."

"Oh?"

I went to the window and watched the breeze gently flutter the leaves on the tree. "I'm confused about Bart. I don't know what to think."

"Want to tell me what happened?" she asked softly.

While running a finger over the dirt on the pane, I told her about his caresses in the truck and how uncomfortable I felt. "He's such a nice guy. Everyone likes him. I like him. But—"

She was thoughtful. "Callie, your love life is your business. We can talk as friends. I've been around a few times myself, you know."

I nodded. I liked that she thought of us as friends.

She continued. "It sounds to me as if you're not comfortable with Bart."

I sat down and looked at her earnestly. "That's it. Part of me really likes him, and yet I don't want a relationship now. I think I ought to love Bart because he is such a wonderful guy. But I don't. And yet I feel I should."

"Why?"

"I dunno. It's like I've started something, and so I ought to go through with it. Stick to my decision, that sort of thing. I guess I'm afraid that relationships can go bad, so why start one? I know Bart's a nice guy, but he deserves someone who's not going to mess it up."

"I see. Since you've gone out with Bart as friends a few times and enjoyed yourself, you feel you should go on with the relationship. But because you've seen others break up, you think it's automatically going to happen to you, right? You think you should protect Bart from the monster lurking inside you. I heard a lot of what Callie *should* do, but nothing about what Callie wants to do." She tilted her head and smiled slightly, but watched me intently.

I grinned, now a little embarrassed after hearing how silly I sounded. Really, Bart and I got along well; it was easy to be myself with him. When I was with him, I felt confident in myself and sure of what to do. Except when our relationship became romantic. I just didn't feel ready to be that involved with anyone now. After hearing it out of Frankie's mouth, I could see that I wasn't paying any attention to what I wanted. "I guess I haven't been very fair with myself."

She tilted her kind face to one side. "Like I've said,

you have good instincts. If I were you, ı'd listen to my own heart." I liked that in Frankie. She didn't try to tell me how to live. I knew she wouldn't give me any more advice, but I also knew how I was going to handle it. Bart would simply have to understand.

She grabbed the pillow on the bed and put it between her back and the wall. "So what else is going on with you? It seems we needed to talk."

I rolled my eyes and laughed. "I guess I have been saving a few stories."

"How's your work going at the site?"

I sighed. "Terrible. I haven't found a thing. I mean, not even a piece of worked flint. Nothing. And I can tell Dr. Petersen is disappointed."

"You don't think he's disappointed in you, do you? You don't have anything to do with what is buried there or not."

"I don't know. Maybe he's just disappointed *for* me. He was so excited to find a student interested in archaeology, and now I haven't turned up anything."

"I'll bet that happened to him a time or two during his student days."

"Maybe, but I don't feel any better. He and his graduate students were hounding me to make sure I'd excavated correctly. Now they are leaving me alone and concentrating on helping those who have discovered something too important to damage."

"What made you pick that square?"

I shrugged as I remembered the eagle feather. "I guess it was a whim. Next time I'll know to study the site more closely."

"At least you're willing to give it another try. That's good."

"It hasn't been dull out there, anyway. We had another incident last evening."

She sat up. "I hadn't heard about that."

I motioned her to sit back. "It was ok, nothing like

104

the first time. In fact, I think Erica and Nick actually prevented it from being more than just a lot of noise."

She arched an eyebrow.

"They were off in the woods having a hot time when all the commotion started. It began at dusk, like last time. Dr. Petersen shouted into the woods, telling off whoever it was, when along came Erica and Nick, still buttoning their clothes. Of course, her dad was furious, but she smugly told him how they had seen someone in the woods. Apparently the guy ran off when he spotted them."

Frankie shook her head. "That Erica is something else. I don't think I'd want to be her mother."

I opened my mouth, about to tell her what I had overheard from Dale and Karen, but then shut it again. It would be a rumor, and I didn't want to cause any more bad feelings between the Petersens and Dr. Broussard.

"What were you going to say?"

"Oh, nothing."

She frowned. "Spit it out. This sounds like something I ought to hear."

"I don't know if it's even true. I just overheard it." She motioned me on. "Ok. Today I heard Dr. Petersen's graduate students say that he had blamed Dr. Broussard for the things that were happening. I didn't want to mention it to you because I don't want things to get worse between them on my account. But I talked to Bart about how jumpy his dad's getting, and asked him if he thought his dad might deliberately ruin the excavation to punish himself—you know, for something wrong he thought he had done in the past. Bart thought he just wasn't the type to do that."

"What made you think that he might be?"

"Well, Dale and Karen think he has been acting weird lately, and you mentioned that he did some strange things in class. And someone else mentioned that all these events that have been going on—the threats—might be the work of someone who was a little crazy."

"I see. I guess it's possible. Do you think Dr. Petersen has been behaving strangely?"

"Now that I think about it, I guess not. I mean, anyone would be upset by these things."

She stared at the ceiling. "I don't know. It's hard for me to say anything about Walt and Jon. Their relationship has been tense for years, according to Walt. Jon has definitely done some unconventional things, but sabotage a project he has worked for years to get under way? I don't think so. And as far as his blaming Walt for things, that sounds like the words of someone under pressure ready to blame an old competitor."

Somewhere in the house, a door slammed.

Frankie stood. "I've got to go to the store. Do you need anything at the pharmacy?"

I shook my head. "You sick?"

"Nope. I'm off to buy a pack of birth control pills."

"No children, huh?"

She looked thoughtful. "I'm getting too old to consider having one—it would be risky at my age. He's never mentioned a desire for kids, and anyway, I don't know how we could handle it with both of us working. I don't think my department would be too eager for me to take time off since we're so short staffed. Besides, I'm just not the mother type." She smiled at me. "I'm better as a big sister or an aunt."

I wondered what the "mother type" was. But I was sure that Frankie had more of it than Mother did.

We heard Dr. Broussard whistling down the hall. He poked his head in my room. "Good evening, ladies. I hope you each had a good day."

He came in and gave Frankie a big kiss.

"My, you're in good spirits," she replied.

He cocked his graying head. "That's the way to say it, good spirits! I'm going to change clothes and then light the barbecue. I thought I'd throw some burgers on the grill, if you didn't have anything else planned, my love."

We laughed. Frankie rarely cooked anything. She forced a serious face. "Well, I was planning veal cordon bleu, but I suppose we can have it another night."

"Yes, let's," he replied with mock gravity, and went to their room to change his clothes.

I stood alone on the center of a small hill. The sky was dark with heavy thunderheads. Lightning stabbed the sky, and I could feel the electrical charge building around me. Wind whipped my hair into knots, tossing strands into my mouth and eyes. I fought to push it back.

High in the sky, with strangely sharp vision, I saw an eagle flying. Its eyes glowed red and I could feel its hatred of me. With a small move of its wings and a determined expression, it dove toward me, talons outstretched. I put my arms above my face to prepare for the attack.

As it sailed down, it grew until it was huge and I was the size of a field mouse in proportion. I hit the ground a split second before it seized me, but it succeeding in ripping away some of my hair. I screamed in agony as I felt the thousand hairs tearing away.

A crash awakened me and I sat up with a lurch, my heart beating furiously, my breaths coming in gasps.

It took me a moment to grasp my surroundings. I was in my bed in the middle of the night. I turned to check the clock and saw that the window was open, the curtains flapping viciously. With a particularly violent snap, I saw that they must have flung the lamp to the floor. A pounding spot on my skull indicated it had hit me first; the incident had worked its way into my dream as hair pulling from my scalp.

"So that's what woke me," I said to myself, trying to force a calm.

I leaned over to pick up the lamp. The bulb had broken, but the rest of it seemed ok.

It was only then that my mind came to a full awareness. "What is the window doing open?" I knew I hadn't opened it before going to bed. It had been too humid outside earlier in the evening for us to eat our hamburgers in the backyard. We had retreated to the air-conditioning.

My eyes fixed on the blowing curtains while an inner dread opened my panic doors. "Close the window! You must close the window, Callie," my mind screamed at me.

I forced my shaking legs onto the floor, but froze as a soft sound began to fill the breeze. A distant chant grew stronger each moment.

In my panic, I couldn't decide what to do. "I'm dreaming this," I whispered, stifling the impulse to run into Frankie's room like a child to its mother's arms.

The chant gradually became audible. "Wasichu, Wasichu. We have come for you."

Despite the wind, I felt hot, and my throat tightened so that it was hard to swallow. I panted.

"Wasichu, we are the Caddo animus. You have violated our holy ground, and we have come for our vengeance. We will pierce your skin as you have pierced the earth. We will peel away your flesh as you have peeled away the dirt which covers us. We will disembowel you slowly, as you have disemboweled us. Come to us, Wasichu."

Although part of my mind froze, the other part wondered what face was behind the voice. "I have to shut the window," I told myself, and so stood, took a step toward the snapping drapes. My senses were acutely tuned: each fiber in the carpet pressed with sharp definition against my feet. The humid night air rushed against my face with a pleasant warmth and an acidic scent of the distant pines. I could hear each portion of the drapery hems moving in a whipping motion. The faint light from a distant street lamp distorted all color to shades of gray and darker gray. I put out my hand and touched the cool window, finding the ledge in need of dusting.

Before I could close it, I raised my eyes from the ledge, past the parting curtains to the contorted, wildly painted face mostly in shadow on the other side of the pane. The eyes, though I could not distinguish their color, were filled with a hysterical, deadly evil. The strangeness and the sense of power in them allured me, probably in the same way that anyone has ever been drawn to true evil. My eyes focused so firmly on his that both pairs appeared to be at each end of a tunnel.

I heard him whisper rather than saw his mouth move. "It is time for the ceremony. You must come. It is time for the sacrifice to be made. The spirits must be appeased."

There was something enchanting about the voice, something that compelled me to do its bidding. For a moment, I wanted to respond, to crawl out the window, a willing victim as if caught in bonds too sweet to desire release.

I screamed. Again, the other half of my mind awoke. "Shut the window, Callie!" Again, I felt the cold dirt on the metal frame, but this time my fingers pressed down. I felt the window move a fraction of an inch and increased the pressure, though my eyes had not left his.

A slow screech began from deep inside him, the eyes trembled in fury. And for a moment, he broke his visual hold on me and glanced down at the window. I looked down, too, and with a shock realized that the screen was off. There was only a pane of glass between this thing and me.

Almost in slow motion I saw him reach with both hands for the underside of the window, and I responded by placing both palms on the ledge and straining down.

I grunted with effort as I tried to force the window closed. He knelt down for better leverage.

It was then that I saw his full body. His clothes were a fringed buckskin shirt and long pants with beaded moccasins. They were neat, almost new. His hair was dark with light streaks, but I couldn't tell if the lightness was a reflection or not. His face was painted in streaks and zigzags. Something was odd about it, and it was not just the grimace as he forced his strength against mine. The shape was not Indian. The bone structure was too narrow and fine, even though the cheeks were full. He seemed vaguely familiar.

As the realization hit me that this was a white man and not Native American, his eyes caught mine. He understood that I had discovered something.

He yelled with a blood chilling screech and shoved with an almost inhuman effort.

"NO!" I shouted, and slammed my weight down on the window. With the benefit of gravity, it eased down lower and lower until he lost his leverage. The window slammed shut, catching his fingers. He screamed, and yet I didn't dare let up the pressure. With one final jerk, he wrenched his fingers free and fled. I threw the lock closed and drew the drapes. I stepped back, clutched myself and gasped for air.

Someone pounded on my door. I whirled around and screamed.

Frankie flipped on the light. "My God, Callie, what's going on?"

I ran to her and grabbed her, my whole body shaking as I clung.

She reached her arms around me and led me over to the bed.

"What's wrong? I heard screams. Did you have a nightmare?"

I shook my head. "Call 911. A man tried to break in here. He was dressed like an Indian. He wanted to kill me!"

Frankie stood and immediately went to the window. "I don't see anyone now, but we'd better call the police. I'll tell Walt. Will you be ok here for a minute?"

110

I didn't want her to leave, but nodded. In a few moments she came back.

"Walt was awakened, too, but he didn't recognize the sound as a scream. He's in the bathroom and will call the police as soon as he comes out. In the meantime, he suggested I make us some cocoa to settle us all down. Let's go into the kitchen."

The light in the kitchen seemed friendly, though I kept glancing toward the window over the sink. Frankie stood in front of the stove in her white cotton gown, her pale bare legs and feet sticking out below. She stirred the cocoa, saying that she still preferred to do it on the stove instead of the microwave. She thought it tasted better.

By the time it was ready, Dr. Broussard entered the door wearing his robe. He hunched his shoulders and had his hands in his pockets and yawned. With only one eye open, and that only a crack, he said sleepily, "The police said they'll search the neighborhood, but figure the guy is long gone by now. They said they'll keep a patrol car by here all night, so you can rest easy. I took a look around outside, but I didn't see anything."

Frankie was pouring the cocoa into mugs. "Want some, honey?"

He yawned so loudly that I contagiously yawned in response. "No, thanks, dear. Oddly enough, I don't think I'll need any help falling back to sleep. I've got a big day ahead tomorrow. Is there anything else I can do?"

I smiled gratefully at him, knowing I wouldn't have stepped foot outside now. "I'll be all right. The cocoa was a good idea. Thanks."

Frankie pecked him on the cheek. "You go on to bed. We'll finish our cocoa and when we feel tired and a bit less nervous, we'll hit the hay, too."

Still leaning against the door frame, he waved at me with his pocketed hand and stumbled into the hall. I heard his slippers flip-flopping to his room.

I breathed in the rich chocolate smell as I swirled the mug in front of my nose. Suddenly, I realized that the person in the window was the same man who had attacked Mother and me that first evening in Weches.

Frankie stood and went to the sink to wash out her cup. I opened my mouth to tell her and then decided against it. No, I didn't want to bother her any more tonight. It could wait till tomorrow.

I remembered the struggle of trying to force the window to close. How did it get open in the first place? Was it unlocked all this time? I saw the ledge of the window again in my mind, pushing, pushing. And then with a jerk, it closed on the intruder's hands.

Frankie stood in the same place where Dr. Broussard had stood moments before. She groped for pockets in which to rest her hands, then realized she did not have on her robe, only her nightgown.

Pockets hide hands.

"Is something wrong?" Frankie asked.

I shook my head to clear it. It was late. I was letting my imagination run wild. "No. I'm tired and I'm starting to imagine all sorts of things. I think it's time to go to bed."

I turned off the kitchen light and followed her down the hall to my room, where we said good night again.

I went inside my room and closed the door. I hesitated in the darkness, and then locked the doorknob.

Twelve

Up at my usual time, I dreaded going into the other part of the house. My night shirt fell to the floor as I reached for some shorts and a plaid blouse. I struggled with a brush through my kinky hair, then settled on wearing it up off my neck.

When I crossed the hall to the bathroom, I locked the door. In five minutes, nothing was left to be done. The smell of bacon frying drifted under the door. My stomach growled, and I knew I couldn't hide in here forever.

"You're being silly," I thought. "Something frightens you in the middle of the night, and all of a sudden you're hunting for ghosts in every corner. Grow up, Callie."

I set my shoulders back and walked into the kitchen. Frankie was turning bacon in the pan, a bright red apron covering her earth-print blouse and khaki skirt.

"Morning, Callie. Did you sleep?"

"After a while. Some night, huh?"

She nodded. "Walt flagged down a patrol car this morning when he went out for the paper. They said they haven't seen anything, but that they would keep a close eye on the house for the next few days. Walt said that if you see anything suspicious, you need to be sure to let us know so that we can report it to the police. And he also suggested that I drive you to campus. He thinks if there is some weirdo after you, you will be safer not riding the bike."

Taking a glass from the shelf, I poured some orange juice and silently chided myself for my suspicions about Dr. Broussard. "If Dr. Broussard were the attacker, he wouldn't care about my safety."

After breakfast Frankie drove me to campus. As I got out at the bus stop, she said, "Now you try to get a ride home with somebody. If you can't, call me and I'll come and pick you up. Have a good day. And be careful."

I watched the bus pull into the parking lot and the sleepy students shuffle into a ragged line in the warm morning sun. Without intending to, I found myself trying to remember all I could about the man's shadowed face last night. "I think I ought to know him," I whispered. "There was something familiar about him, but I don't know if it's my imagination, or if I'm simply remembering the first time I saw him."

Somehow, it was if my brain was trying to tell me something, but I wasn't yet able to understand it. But it felt important, and I knew I shouldn't ignore it.

In the bus, my regular seat was vacant. Erica was flirting with Nick as always, though she paused at one point and gave me a brief, bashful smile, and I nodded. Apparently things had permanently changed between us, though I could see it would take a lot of work on my part if we were to become true friends. I wasn't even sure I wanted to be close friends with her, though I was glad to be a little more comfortable around her. Still, Erica wasn't my type.

I used the trip to look over my notebook, noting pages where I needed to explain myself further or more neatly re-draw sketches. Karen would grade my work in the next couple of days, and I wanted to do as well as I could.

Before we broke up to go to our stations around the site, Dale lectured us on the importance of cleaning our tools each night to prevent rusting and assure a longer tool life. We listened impatiently, and then were released.

I gathered my tools from a box in back of the bus and walked across the balks to my square. The area was taking on quite a professional appearance to it. I glanced at several square floors, thinking how they looked like photos from *National Geographic.*

With another sigh, I crawled into my fruitless square and took up the trowel. There was another large stone off to one side, and I knelt down by it. As I worked to remove it, I fantasized about what might be on the other side of it. Maybe there would be a carving on the underside. I snorted. "Ha. Dreams of glory, eh Callie? Face it. All you're going to find is another big rock, and more dirt. That's part of archaeology, too, to find the limits of the site."

It took me thirty minutes or more of patient work to remove it. It was jagged and larger than it had first appeared. At last it loosened its grip on the dirt. I pried it out carefully as I had learned.

Lifting it in my hands, I turned it around. Yup. Another big rock. Disappointed, I set it on the balk. I figured I'd wait until I had several before I hauled it off.

I went back to the hole in the floor. A chunk of red clay had loosened as the rock had come out, and I reached in and removed it.

Underneath was something white. My heart seemed to skip a beat. I reached for my trowel and tapped it gently. It wasn't rock, too soft for that, but it was hard.

You'd better not yell until you're sure.

Working quickly, but carefully, I removed the dirt and clay above it. I forced myself to do it neatly and level the surrounding floor as I dug.

Again, I felt someone watching me. I looked up from my work and saw that Dr. Petersen was interested in my sudden spurt of activity. I couldn't help but smile, but did not motion him over. He said something to Dale, then headed in my direction. I went back to work.

Dr. Petersen didn't say anything as he arrived but watched me remove the next layer. He squatted on his haunches.

At last I was down to the level which I had intended. I worked around the small patch of white, now with my hands, now with a brush.

In a short time, it was plain that I was uncovering a long heavy bone, probably from the thigh of a good-sized animal.

Taking off my sunglasses and wiping the bridge of my nose, I cocked my head to him. "So do you think it's human?"

He nodded, but wasn't smiling the way he had with the other big finds. He eased himself onto the floor of the square, and I hopped out to give him more room.

He took the brush laying beside the bone and swept away a bit more of the crumbled earth. He stopped and scratched his chin. He spoke at the bone. "I'd say you've found something very significant," he began.

I could feel my chest filling with pride. After so much discouragement, something really important.

He ran his fingers over the exposed area. "This explains a lot. Now I know why we were threatened so much. Somebody had a good reason. He knew about this."

I was puzzled. "How could somebody know what was buried here? You are the expert on this site, and you didn't know it was here."

He stood and sat on the opposite balk, still looking at the bone. "This is recent, Callie. It's not from the same period as the rest of the finds."

"Recent? How can you tell? I thought you said I'd found a very significant artifact."

He shook his head, took off his cap and ran his fingers through his sweaty blond hair. He sighed and looked at me. Bart had his father's eyes.

116

"Callie, these bones are recent. Very recent, as in the last few years. Somebody buried a dead body on the site, and now he's afraid we'll discover him."

"How can you be sure?" His words were hitting with that ring of truth with which I was becoming uncomfortably familiar.

He nodded over his shoulder. "Compare floor depths. Yours is the most shallow." He indicated one of my balks. "And your walls don't show the same pattern of soil deposition. They look as if the dirt had been churned up."

I was about to protest, but he waved me silent. "But the thing that tells me the most—the damning evidence, you might say—is the color of the bones. They're too white. There isn't any sign that the minerals in the surrounding soil have begun to replace the calcium, as you would expect if they had been buried for a long time."

"Why would anyone bury someone out here without marking the grave, unless they didn't want anyone else to find the body? And why would you hide a body . . . ?" We looked at each other in silence.

"Callie, I don't want you talking to any of the other students about this. Continue to remove the dirt, but don't move this bone or any other you find. I'll tell Karen and Dale to see to it that you aren't disturbed."

"You're going to the police?"

He nodded. "I'm going directly to the County Medical Examiner's office. He's a friend of mine. I'm sure the sheriff's department will follow us out here."

He pulled his lean, tanned body out of the square and crossed stakes, strings and balks to where Karen was discussing a pottery fragment with another student. He motioned her away, speaking with a few nods in my direction. Her face grew worried and also turned my way. She dug in her khaki shorts' pocket for her car keys and handed them to Dr. Petersen. He left without another word.

117

Karen walked over to the large sifter, took Dale back a few steps, and repeated Dr. Petersen's motions. He nodded and went back to the sifter, while she headed my way.

She squatted on the balk in a line between the sun and me, giving me some much appreciated shade. "Mind if I take a closer look?"

"Sure." We switched places. She rubbed her fingers over the bone, then using a toothbrush, began to remove more of the dirt covering it. She exposed another three inches, then stopped, handing the toothbrush to me. "Wonder who the poor bastard was?" she muttered, getting out of the square.

I twisted the toothbrush in my hand. "I hope whoever it was has been buried for a long time. I'd hate to find . . ."

She placed her hand on my shoulder reassuringly. "Don't worry. From the looks of things, you won't find any partially decomposed soft tissue. Besides, chances are the coroner will take over the square after he arrives anyway."

I rolled my eyes. "Oh, great. This has been excellent field experience in archaeology for me."

She shrugged sympathetically. "I'll be staying on this half of the site. If anyone wants to talk to you, they'll have to produce their notebook to be graded first."

"That ought to keep the visitors down."

"That's the idea."

For the rest of the morning, I carefully exposed first one bone, then another, being sure to leave supporting dirt under each one. The skeleton was an adult curled into a fetal position, just like the Caddoes used to bury their dead. I was exposing the left side: the femur, patella, fibula and tibia, and tarsus. I left the rest of the left foot covered; I didn't know if all those little bones would fall apart or not.

I began again at the top of the femur and worked at

uncovering a good portion of the pelvis. At least it was now apparent that the bones were not scattered.

Concentrating on removing flecks of dirt from the exposed pelvis, I didn't hear the cars pull up or anyone approaching until they were very close by. I peered over the top of the balk and saw Dr. Petersen leading two men in civilian clothing and two uniformed officers across the network of walls toward me. All work had stopped, and students were collecting in groups of threes and fours across the site. Erica caught my eye with questions on her face, but I shrugged and indicated I'd have to talk to the approaching men.

As Dr. Petersen reached my square, he turned to the students. "Everyone back to work. You've all got enough to do, or if not, I can arrange a pop quiz to keep you busy." With groans and curled lips, they slowly responded to his command, obviously wanting to know what was happening.

"Gentlemen, I'd like to introduce you to the student who discovered the remains, Callie Davis. Callie, this is Roger Bailey, Weches County Sheriff, and Dr. Gary Thomas, County Medical Examiner. The coroner will be here later."

I dusted off my hand on my shorts and stuck it out to the first man, who was around forty, overweight, and wearing a crew cut. He took my hand in his plump one and shook it firmly.

"How do you do, sir," I said.

"How do, ma'am."

I watched from the balk as the doctor and sheriff examined what I had done and the condition of the bones.

Dr. Petersen winked at me. "As I explained to you in the car, because of the location of the remains, I want to disturb the surrounding soil as little as possible. I think an archaeologist should do the actual excavating, with your professional supervision, of course."

The sheriff stood up and pulled his pants up by the belt to a higher position on his belly. "You gonna do this, Jon?"

Dr. Petersen shook his head. "Callie knows this particular spot better than I do. She's been working on it for weeks. She'd more quickly spot any changes in soil texture or any other anomalies. And I think you'll agree she's done a fine job so far."

"Don't make me no nevermind," Bailey replied. "You, Doc?"

The young medical examiner smiled at me. "If she wants to get her hands dirty, that's fine with me."

The thought of rotten remains sobered me. "I'd be glad to help. I've been the only one out here who hasn't discovered something. Say, Dr. Thomas? You don't think I'll find—"

He laughed. "—worms crawling in and out the dead man's snout? No, I don't think so. You may find buttons and zippers, that sort of thing. Maybe some hair. But nothing to turn your stomach. And by the way, it's a she, not a he."

"You can tell that already?"

"The pelvis. Women have a wider pelvis. We'll discover more as you go on."

I continued to work, a bit nervously at first, and then gradually became used to my audience. I even put them to work hauling away the dirt to the sifter.

Bailey ordered the officers to scout the area, and then to station themselves on either side of the site. I noticed they kept their holsters unsnapped and guns ready.

I would have enjoyed the attention which I was no doubt receiving from the rest of the class, but I was too involved in what I was doing. Bailey read through my notebook and indicated he wanted to take it in and make official copies of it.

"We may need to keep it for evidence and give you the copies. Think you would mind copying the information over into another notebook? We'd supply it for you."

"Sure. I don't mind. I don't see that there's much in there that you would find important."

He flipped back to the front. "Says here you chose the square because there was an eagle feather on it. Want to explain that?"

I was working on separating each rib from the other. I had been meaning to erase that sentence before it was graded. I took a deep breath and told him about seeing Manitu Flying Eagle. I told him about the frightening events at the site, at the University and at home. "I guess it had something to do with the shaman's name and her warning. It seemed like the right place to choose. And the next day, when we came back to the site, the feather was gone. I suppose it blew away."

Bailey frowned as he stopped taking notes. "It seems there has been a great deal more goin' on with y'all than first appeared. I think I need to talk to Jon. But you don't go away. You and I need to have a longer talk, young lady."

I hoped I hadn't gotten Dr. Petersen in trouble, but the visitor in my window had shaken me.

About four o'clock we stopped to rest, and I finally ate lunch. I relished the relative cool of the shade, feeling every breath of wind speed the cooling of my body. Dr. Thomas remained at my square and continued to work.

Erica casually wandered over to the large water jug and then on to me. "Having a busy day, huh? The police look into the hole and bring the medical examiner. It's not for a pot. You've found a dead body—what our night visitor hoped to scare us away from." Her voice grew frightened.

I glanced around quickly. "Ssh. We're not even supposed to be talking."

She furrowed her brow. "Callie, this crazy man has killed once and he can do it again. You must be careful. Oh, God. He's likely to want to kill you now that you

121

have uncovered his secret. You must promise me to be very, very careful. Never be alone. Promise?" She grasped my arm firmly.

My mouth nearly dropped open in my surprise at her ability to be so observant. After all, she played the part of a bimbo, but the seriousness of her face stopped me. I simply nodded. One of the officers had spotted us talking and was heading toward us. I motioned Erica away. "It's ok," I called to the policeman. "She's my friend and she was worried about me. I didn't tell her anything."

Karen and Dale stopped the work early and ordered everyone back on the bus. Within ten minutes, the equipment had been put up and the bus loaded. They left, leaving Karen's car behind for our use.

I went back to work. At Dr. Thomas's suggestion, I sped up the process without damaging the surrounding soil layers. The left half of the body was completely exposed now, but we realized that the skull was missing.

"Somehow, I'm not surprised," Dr. Thomas said, referring to the attacker's bizarre behavior.

As the sun began to set, one of the officers brought out some portable lights from the trunk of a squad car. Although the lights allowed us to continue, now I batted moths away.

As the darkness crept across the sky, I picked up my head and listened into the wind.

"What is it?" Bailey asked, his heavy body brought to full attention.

Listening closer, I could barely make out rhythmical sounds. I whispered. "I think we're going to have a visitor again."

Bailey clicked his fingers and whistled quietly. I couldn't see the officers, but assumed they had moved out of sight. Dr. Petersen joined us.

Bailey reached down to his ankle and unstrapped a small pistol. "You know how to use one of these, Jon?

Doc here refuses to touch 'em."

"As a graduate student in the jungles of Central America I shot a couple of snakes. But it's been a long time."

"Once is better than nonce, as I always say." He turned the pistol around and pointed to the safety. "When this is off, keep it pointed to the ground, got it? I think it would be better if each of you stayed at the bottom of one of these holes with the lights out. As you are, you're perfect targets. Callie, you're the least likely to crush the evidence, so you stay in your square. Jon you go here and Doc over there with the lights. And Doc, if you hear anything at all, flood those lights in that direction."

"That's a roger, Roger," Doc said with a smile at the corner of his mouth. They left to their respective squares and the lights went out.

Bailey was still close by. "Jon, you make sure you get a good look at something before you shoot at it. You could be hittin' me or one of my men. I got days off comin', and want to spend 'em in a bass boat, not a hospital."

I heard him creep away. The night sounds closed in around me as my hearing became super-acute. I heard a night bird fluttering near the trees. An owl hooted in the middle of its silent flight directly above me. The breeze gently ruffled the pine needles all around. I could see the stars clearly, the Milky Way a bright stain across inky paper.

And then he was coming. He slipped out of some trees on the opposite side of the clearing where he had appeared before. I felt like a stalked animal trapped in my hole. I wanted to run. I wanted to shout for help, but was afraid of giving away my position.

I could hear the soft crunch of footsteps, and wondered how he could be so surefooted in this maze. Dr. Thomas, turn the lights on, I willed. The steps grew closer and then stopped within a few feet of me. I looked down, fearing the starlight would reflect in my eyes and give me away.

He screamed a bloodcurdling yell. When I looked up, he lunged toward me. The light flashed on and I saw my window attacker approaching with knife in hand. He stopped, covered his eyes from the light and dashed away.

Dr. Petersen yelled and shot. The figure disappeared into the woods. Bailey and his men ran from the other side of the clearing, one of the officers tripping on a string and sent sprawling in one of the squares. The other two slowed their chase enough to be sure that they wouldn't fall. Dr. Petersen scrambled out of his square.

"Stay DOWN," Bailey shouted as he passed us. Dr. Thomas flashed the light toward the woods.

We waited breathlessly, the three of us still crouching in our holes. The other officer dragged himself out of the square and crouched near us, revolver drawn in both hands and scanning the tree line.

After twenty minutes, Bailey and the policeman returned.

"He got away," Bailey spat, disgusted.

"Who was it?" Dr. Thomas asked.

"Somebody crazy, that's for sure," Dr. Petersen replied.

Dr. Thomas swept the area with the lights once again.

"Hey, shine it over there," I said. I scrambled out of my hole and across the edge of the site to something light colored on the ground. It was a piece of leather thong with an eagle feather attached to it. It had been shot off.

"I guess you got us a clue, Dr. Petersen." I held it up for them to see.

Thirteen

We worked out at the site until late in the evening. Dr. Petersen asked Bailey to radio the dispatcher to call Frankie and tell her I'd be very late and not to worry.

It took me quite a while to uncover the skeleton. We never found the skull.

"Not surprised," Bailey said. "If you want to hide the identity of the victim, it's best to bury the skull some place else. Dental records are as good as fingerprints."

When I completely unearthed the skeleton, Bailey and Dr. Thomas carefully removed it and placed it in a bag inside a wooden box to be taken back to the crime lab.

As Dr. Petersen and I drove home in Karen's car, I became increasingly more nervous about Dr. Broussard. It could all be my imagination, but I didn't want to sleep at Frankie's house. I didn't think I could sleep. How was I supposed to say that I was suspicious of Dr. Broussard without having any proof?

"Ok, what's wrong," Dr. Petersen asked.

I sighed. "I guess I'm just upset about tonight. I'm not looking forward to going into that house alone after everyone's asleep." Especially since I didn't know who'd be lurking there.

"I'm having a hard time understanding why you are being singled out for these attacks now. The threats have stopped as far as I'm concerned. It's had me worried." He looked away from the road to me. "Callie, I know you enjoy your work at the site. You might even want to go into archaeology one day. But I'm concerned about your safety. I'm going to ban you from the excavation, at least for a while. You've done a fine job, and with the excavation of the skeleton, you've done ample work to complete the course with flying colors. You did a very professional job today. I thought you might work in the lab. That part is important, too. In fact, it is really the more advanced work, where we discover exactly what it is we've found and develop the overall view of the site."

He paused, glanced at me again, and I nodded, too disappointed to speak. "Look," he continued. "Let's just play it by ear. We're going to have to close the site tomorrow anyway so that the police can do a thorough search of the area. They may catch the guy, and then we won't have to worry about it. Besides, if it gets any hotter out there, you may be begging me to work in the lab."

I gave him a small smile, knowing he was trying to cheer me up.

"That's better. Say, since it's so late, why don't you come home to our house and sleep over? Bart can take you home tomorrow. A change of pace might do you good."

I kicked off the blanket in the morning light and saw that my blouse and shorts looked as if I had washed them, tied them in knots, then allowed them to dry. "Oh, well." I put them on, then folded the blanket and sheet and stacked them with the pillow on one end of the couch.

I picked up my purse, grateful that I at least kept some make-up and a comb there, and headed for the bathroom.

As I walked down the hall, Bart came out of his room wearing only his underwear.

He was surprised, but then smiled unbashfully and placed his hands on his hips. His muscular but hairless chest was tanned more lightly than his forearms. His blond hair was in complete disarray, but he still looked great in the morning. His attitude was so casual that I felt little different than seeing a brother in underwear. Well, maybe a little different.

"Morning, bright eyes," he said grinning. "Fancy meeting you here."

I kept my eyes on his face. I hoped I wasn't blushing too much. "Morning. How'd you sleep?"

"The better question is how did you sleep? That was quite a night you had."

"Actually, I slept better than I have for a week or more. That couch is comfy."

"Got any plans today? I'm taking the day off."

Again, that uncomfortable feeling gnawed at me about being with him. *I wish I wouldn't feel so confused around him. I'm attracted to him, and yet I don't want to be close. What's wrong with me?* I tried to think up an excuse to keep me busy. I needed to check out my suspicions of Dr. Broussard, but I didn't know how to voice the subject. "I may have some things I need to do, but we can talk after breakfast."

I hurried into the bathroom so no one would catch us talking while he was practically naked. I cleaned my face and brushed my teeth with my finger so my mouth wouldn't taste like sawdust. After putting on some make-up and brushing my hair I looked better, but my rumpled clothes disgusted me.

Bart and I traded places and Erica stepped out of her room in a robe and nightgown. She looked as if someone had sneaked in her room and teased her curls into a wild nest. Her mascara made a black smear under her eyes like a football linebacker. She startled when she saw me.

"Callie. What are you doing here?" She ran her hand over the tangled curls.

"Your dad and the police and I worked late at the site. He suggested I sleep over and go home in the morning."

"What's going on out there? Why were the police called?"

I told her what I had found and her father's conclusion about it. I described the attack last night and how her dad had shot off part of the attacker's headdress.

"Oh, it must have been scary. I'm glad I wasn't there."

"Scary doesn't even come close. Terrifying is the truth."

She examined my clothes and turned up her lip. "You look awful. Why don't you wear something of mine until you can change?"

Comparing the two of us, I nearly laughed. But she was trying to be friendly. "No, that's all right. Thanks."

Her eyes pleaded with me and she lowered her voice. "Come on. I haven't been very fair to you, and it would make me feel better. Besides, Dad's still pretty mad at me for messing around with Nick, and I could use all the help I can get with him."

"Ok. Sure. I'd appreciate it. I do look tacky."

We went to her bedroom, decked with blue ruffles from the canopied bed to the curtains and the vanity.

After a couple of tries, we found a pair of shorts that fit (I was glad to see I had the smaller waist), but I had to settle on a t-shirt, because all her blouses were way too big in the chest. I quietly sighed.

Thirty minutes later everybody was dressed and in the kitchen. Mrs. Petersen, a fading beauty who talked nonstop, barked orders from the stove: "Jon, dear, get me some coffee, please. Bart, set the table. Erica, start the toast. Callie, could you mix the orange juice? You'll find a can in the freezer."

128

When the poached eggs on toast had been eaten and cleared, Mrs. Petersen and Erica left to do some shopping. Dr. Petersen excused himself to go out to the site.

"I don't want any over-efficient officers turning stones where they shouldn't. Callie, I want you to be careful today. If you should see anything suspicious, call the Weches Police."

"Don't worry. Dr. Broussard called them the other night and they said they were going to patrol regularly." Even as I said it, I wondered if he had indeed called them, or if he had only pretended to.

"Good, but you still need to take care. Going to work today, Bart?"

Bart answered to me rather than his father. "Oh, I thought I'd take at least the morning off. I may do some work this afternoon."

His father rattled his keys in his cargo shorts. "Ok, I'm off. No screwing around, you two." He turned on his heels, not waiting for a reply.

"Sorry about that," Bart said as he watched the door to the garage close.

I watched him for a moment, taking in his neat button-down short-sleeved work shirt and blue jeans.

He pushed back his chair vigorously. "I'm at your service. Where would you like to go today?"

I smiled, feeling a little more comfortable with him. I grew more serious. "Actually, I'd like to go see Manitu Flying Eagle again. There seem to be eagle feathers cropping up all over the place. I'd like to see what she thinks about recent events."

"Ok, let's go."

As we drove out of Weches into the rolling pine-covered hills, Bart asked me to explain to him again the events of last night, which I did. He was particularly interested in the attacker.

"Are you sure it was the same man in the window from the night before last?"

129

"Absolutely. A face like that is hard to forget. The pattern of paint on his face was the same, too."

"Did you feel you knew him when you saw him?"

"Not this time. I mean, I'm becoming familiar with him. Besides, I only saw his face a moment in the light before he turned and ran. But the other night at Frankie's, it was his eyes that seemed familiar. It's strange about eyes. They seem to tell so much about what is going on inside a person. Someone can lie to you with words and with their face and actions, but look them in the eye and you'll know."

He nodded, turning down the dirt road to the cabin. "I know what you mean. Maybe he just seemed familiar because he obviously knows you. Maybe your mind is thinking you ought to know him, when in fact you don't."

I hesitated, but couldn't ignore my mind's question mark about Dr. Broussard. "Maybe. I don't know."

We were approaching the cabin, though we couldn't see it yet. I put my hand on his arm. "Slow down. I'd like to surprise anyone there."

He not only slowed down, but pulled to the side of the road and stopped the truck. "Why don't we walk, then?"

When I opened the door, the full force of the Texas summer hit me in waves of heat from the ground and the sun. We closed the doors quietly. I walked around the front and joined Bart in the center of the red dirt road.

"What are you expecting to find," Bart asked quietly. We walked down the gully on the other side of the road and up again to the tree line.

"I don't know. There's something bothering me about our visit last time. Remember how the candles lit at the same time? Candles don't do that by themselves. Call me a skeptic, but I don't believe she did it by magic, either."

He glanced at me. "You know, I hadn't thought of that. So you think she's a fake?"

I shook my head. "I don't know what to think of her. She seemed to know so much about me, and everything she said made sense. She warned me to be careful of everyone around me, and I don't think that sounds like someone who would want to do me harm."

"Yeah, I guess that's true. I've always thought that fortune tellers were fakes, but she was right about you being in danger. She warned me to protect you. I haven't done a very good job of that."

"Oh, come on, Bart. That would be impossible. You can't go to the site with me, and we don't live in the same house. And it's not your responsibility to follow me around like a guard dog. You've got a life of your own."

He didn't respond. We came to the edge of the trees by the dirt drive in front of the cabin. We hid in some brush and studied the place silently.

The windows and door were shut with no lights or signs of life. For five minutes we sat still and heard no sounds besides a mockingbird and the drone of cicadas.

"Of course it looked like this when we drove up before," I said.

"True. What do you want to do?"

I thought a moment. "The guy that attacked me never had a gun that I could see, so maybe we don't have to worry about being shot. Why don't we walk up like we were planning to visit?"

"Ok by me."

We stepped out into the lane and approached the run-down house. Our eyes shifted from side to side while we tried to appear casual. I stepped on the rotten wood porch and a board squeaked. A rat ran out from under the step and passed my other foot still on the grass. I jerked it up in a hurry.

"Nice place," I said.

Bart joined me on the porch, and I stepped up to the door and knocked. No answer. I knocked again. "Miss

Flying Eagle? Hello. Are you there?"

There was no answer.

Bart stepped over to the window which had had a candle in it last time and peered in through the dirty pane. He took off his sunglasses and placed his hand over his eyes to see more clearly. "Nobody home."

I tried the doorknob. It wasn't locked. I shoved it open. "Hello? Miss Flying Eagle? It's Callie Davis."

Still no answer.

I looked at Bart. "I'd like to check inside."

"I'll come with you."

I shook my head. "I don't want someone sneaking up on us. Why don't you check around outside and see what you can find?"

He frowned. "Callie, I don't like splitting up."

"What if somebody comes back? They'll see your truck on the road and suspect we're here. You can talk loudly to give me enough time to slip out the back. If I get in trouble inside, I'll shout, ok?" He didn't move. "Go on, now. Let's hurry before we have company."

He walked away slowly, and I knew he'd stick close to the house. I stepped inside the door and stood still for a moment, allowing my eyes to become adjusted to the dusty gloom.

In the opposite corner, as before, was the old wooden table and three chairs. In places, cracks of sunlight slipped through the wall boards and onto the rough, dusty floor. About three feet up on the wall were supporting beams which the outside logs had been attached to. Every foot or so on the cross beams was a brass candle holder and candles.

I stepped over to the wall by the table.

The candle holder in front of me was made of brass-colored plastic and the candle was fake, too. Where the wick should have been was a small, flame-shaped light bulb. Looking more carefully, I now saw electrical wires running from one candle to another. I followed the cord

132

to the table and down to the chair behind it. Underneath the chair was a taped switch. I threw it on and the "candles" lit simultaneously. I turned it off.

"Hey, what's going on?" I heard Bart say outside.

"It's ok," I called. "Just testing the lights."

I wondered where the electrical hookup was, but suspected a battery was hidden some place, as I hadn't seen power lines run to the house.

I walked outside onto the porch and closed the door, pushing the sunglasses on the top of my head down on my nose. Even so, the bright Texas sunlight caused me to squint. In a moment Bart came from around the back of the house.

"Callie, I found something you might want to see."

Toward the middle of an overgrown garden was a row of wilting plants, their upper stems bent under the weight of the purplish-blue flowers and leaves no longer erect. The gardener hadn't been out to water or to weed.

The flowers. I saw a wilting plant attached to a knife by leather thongs. I saw a listing in a book of herbs headed "Monkshood."

My mind was working fast as I turned to Bart and narrowed my eyes. The man in the forest threw the knife. The knife held an eagle feather and deadly monkshood. Manitu Flying Eagle had a garden in back of her cabin with monkshood growing. The cabin was uninhabited, and looked as if it had not been lived in for years. Dr. Broussard referred me to the shaman. Was this a conspiracy of some sort? Had Dr. Broussard hired these people, or was he working with them to cover up the location of the dead woman's body—who had probably been murdered? Who was she? Why would he be involved with such people? Were they blackmailing him?

"Bart, this doesn't make sense. Everything seems to point back to Dr. Broussard. But why would he be involved with a murder? He's a nice, thoughtful man. He's had some hard times in his life, but he is willing to talk about them, at least to Frankie."

"Everybody has hard times. What does that have to do with it?"

I shrugged and bent down to examine a monkshood blossom more closely. "Manitu Flying Eagle warned me to be careful. She seemed concerned for my welfare. But there was that eagle feather on the Caddo burial mound, as if someone wanted me to discover the body." I noticed he was still looking at me. "Maybe that's it. Maybe someone needed me to discover the body. Maybe they wanted my help to tell about the murder."

He didn't respond. "I don't know what to think about this, Callie. What did you find in the cabin?"

"Nothing, except that the candles were an electrical setup. The shaman used them for effect."

"Fake, just like I thought."

"But how did she know so much about me?"

He stretched his hand to me and helped me to my feet. "I don't know. I'm confused. Things aren't making sense. It's crazy."

As we walked back to the truck, I thought about Dr. Broussard. He was so likable, but kept himself distant. I could tell that he sincerely liked me.

We climbed into the truck and started the engine. Bart rolled down his window to let out the baked heat from inside and flicked the air conditioner fan on high. "Where to now?"

"Why don't you take me home? I'd like to talk to Frankie about Dr. Broussard. Maybe he's in some sort of trouble. Maybe not. But I'd like to learn more about him."

On the way back to town, my thoughts absorbed me. Why would Dr. Broussard have anything to do with a fake shaman? Maybe he didn't know she was a fake. Or maybe she wasn't fake. Maybe she was simply using the cabin on occasion. And of course he's interested in folklore and the like. Why would he associate with the madman dressed as an Indian? Or more likely, they didn't have anything to do with each other. Perhaps this wild man was behind it all.

I drifted from puzzle to puzzle, not arriving at any conclusions, but creating more questions. Only when Bart pulled onto Frankie's street did I come back to the present.

"You've got company," Bart said.

In the driveway was a Weches County Sheriff's car. Sheriff Bailey walked back from the front door of the house, opened the police car, then spotted us pulling into the driveway behind him.

"Callie? Just came to talk to you, girl." He looked at Bart questioningly.

"Oh, sorry. Roger Bailey, this is Bart Petersen, Dr. Petersen's son."

"How do, young man. You don't mind if I talk to your girlfriend, here, do you? Matter of official business." His rumpled brown pants sagged under the weight of his stomach and his dingy white shirt had perspiration stains under the arms.

"Glad to meet you sir," Bart replied. He turned to me. "Guess I'll leave you. I'm going back to work, but you call if you need anything, ok?"

I smiled at his earnest concern. "Sure." I watched him leave and waved as he drove down the street. Reaching in my pocket, I dug out a house key. We went into the living room and I invited Sheriff Bailey to have a seat on the large beige sofa. I got us some Cokes from the kitchen.

"Thanks. Hot day." He downed his Coke quickly, but didn't want another. "Guess I didn't really need to chase the Petersen boy off, but didn't want to spread any rumors around."

"It's ok. What's up?"

He dug inside a cheap briefcase and produced a thick folded stack of xerox copies. "I talked to the D.A. and he said he'd like to keep your notebook. Gave Jon some money to buy you another one, and he said he'd see you get it. Sorry about the extra work."

"Oh, it won't take long to copy all this into another book. Actually, I wanted to make the drawings neater anyway."

"Good. By the way, Doc's had a chance to examine the remains more closely. The body is that of a Caucasian female, late-twenties to early-thirties, no children."

"How can you tell she didn't have any children?"

"Bone structure changes when you have a kid. But that's not the most important thing. She was murdered."

I nodded. "I figured as much. Why else would anybody go to so much trouble to hide a body and to try to scare everyone off?"

He grinned at me. "You're thinking like a cop, kid. But you're right. Doc found several knife marks on the ribs indicating she had been stabbed to death repeatedly. That's a violent way to go. The killer was venting a lot of frustration on this woman."

"Was she—"

"Raped? Can't say for certain now, but probably not. She was buried with care. That indicates it was someone who knew and cared for her."

"Anything else you learned?" I was amazed that a dead body could tell so much.

"Sure. She was roughly 5 feet 7 inches and 125 pounds. We don't know her hair color. That's another thing. The killer was smart. He knew that he might be caught some day, so he hid her skull some place else so that we couldn't identify her. We also know that she died five to seven years ago."

"Do the police files show any women missing at that time?"

He snorted. "Sure. Hundreds, from all over the country. But she was buried in an Indian historical site. That's significant. The site was probably important to the killer,

136

or he knew it was important to the victim. And they were probably from around these parts. We're checking on leads now."

He stood to go. "Now Callie, I don't want you running around alone. For some reason, this crazy guy thinks you're to blame for the discovery of the body. I'm going to see to it that the house is watched, especially at night, which that weirdo seems to prefer."

I nodded. "The city police have already been keeping an eye on the place since my late night visitor the night before last."

He arched an eyebrow. "Oh? They didn't tell me. City and county don't always act as if they're on the same side. I'll check into it and make sure we're not duplicating anything. Can I use your phone?"

I led him into the kitchen, where he called the city police department.

"You sure? Maybe you guys just don't do your paperwork very quickly. No, I'm positive. I've got somebody from that household here who says they called you. All right, all right. I just called to make sure we didn't waste manpower by having city and county run cars by here. You do that, and get back to me. I don't want this little girl scared at night any more." He winked at me. "Fine. You know where to reach me." He hung up.

"You wouldn't believe how many things get messed up because the paperwork's not done. Dispatcher says she doesn't have any record of the patrols on your house, but she's going to check with the officers on the shift and put a fire under 'em." He walked to the door. "Now, you call me if you see anything troubling, or think of anything else you should tell me."

I thought about my suspicions about Dr. Broussard being in trouble. I just couldn't tell him that and get Dr. Broussard in hot water when I could be wrong. It could ruin his reputation.

137

I had an idea. I'd check around here for any clues, then give Bailey a call if I found anything at all. "Sure, I'll call you," I said, feeling more confident now that I had a plan.

Standing at the curtained living room windows, I watched him drive away. For the first time in two days, I was alone.

Fourteen

I turned back to the living room and became keenly aware of the silence in the house. Inside, I felt a growing paranoia. "Am I truly alone?"

At ten years old, when Mother and Dad were not at home, I would go through the whole house checking in every closet, under every bed and behind each shower curtain to assure myself that nothing lurked in a hidden corner. The same compulsion overcame me now, and I began a methodical search of the house, beginning with the living room, kitchen, den, and then Frankie and Walt's study. They generally kept the door closed to this last room. I peered in, seeing the standard mess everywhere.

"It's almost like a sanctuary to Walt and me," Frankie had explained one time. "It's for our private use, though we rarely go there together. If I'm reading a selection of articles from a stack of books, why should I have to put them back in the shelves if I don't finish? I leave them beside the stuffed chair on the table for the next time."

All four walls in this room were covered with floor-to-ceiling bookcases which were filled with generally neat rows of books. They obviously liked to be able to find their books again after they were through with them. I tried the door to the closet—the room was originally a bedroom—and found that it was locked.

I searched my room and closet and went to their bedroom. I hesitated before the door, but when my nerves couldn't stand the suspense any longer, I walked in. I looked under their neatly made king-size bed, and then went into the bathroom. It was small, trimmed in peach and blue. There was a good-sized frosted window over the john with gathered peach curtains. I opened the shower, stuck my head in, and then closed it. I looked back at the window. It was large enough for a man to crawl in and out of when he needed a discreet exit, like if he wanted to scare another person in the house at her bedroom window.

I was beginning to feel guilty and foolish for this charade, but the obsession wouldn't leave me, so I continued.

Frankie's closet was not the neatest I had seen, with clothes hanging crookedly from their hangers. The floor didn't have any clothes wadded on it, just piles of mismatched shoes.

That left Dr. Broussard's closet. I hesitated before it, took a deep breath, and opened it.

I don't know what I expected to find, but I didn't see anything spectacular. I turned on the light and walked in.

He was neater than Frankie. His slacks were hanging together on one side, followed by jackets and coats. On the other side rows of shirts hung neatly. His matched shoes lay at precise intervals under his shirts on the carpeted floor. On the back wall of the closet was a necktie rack thick with ties. But it was hung at about waist level, so that many of the ties touched the floor.

"Hm." I ran my hand underneath, enjoying the smooth coolness of their silky texture.

I glimpsed something behind them. I knelt and pushed the ties aside with my arm. A small paneled door had been hidden behind them. My heart pounded. I knew what was on the other side. The study was the room next to theirs; mine was on the other side of the hall. And the locked closet was on the other side of the wall next to this one.

I carefully pulled the door open, and saw that the ties which would have been pulled off most frequently had been sewn onto their pegs. I couldn't see anything through the opening. Shaking on the inside, I knew I had to find out what was in that closet. I knew intuitively that some answers lay there.

Breathing shallowly like a panicked animal, I crawled through the small door into the dark, feeling my way with my hands.

The floor inside the other closet was carpeted. I couldn't see light from underneath the opposite door, so I assumed that the edges had been covered to prevent light from escaping. Would I have to escape from this room?

I lifted my knees over the low sill of the small door and sat in what I thought was the center of the other closet. Allowing my eyes to become adjusted to the dim light coming from the hole to Dr. Broussard's closet, I forced myself to take steady breaths. I willed my body to relax, my mind to still, and I felt the panic receding, though I could tell I had erected only a temporary wall to hold back the fear. My eyes focused on the area around me. Seeing a candle and matches on a low box, I ripped a stick from the book and struck it, lighting the wick. The flame stretched tall and bright.

Next to the candle was a clear plastic tray filled with different colored powders. Closer examination of a label on the corner read "Stagelight Cosmetics."

On hangers above me was a buckskin outfit, followed by a feathered Native American headdress. I reached up and touched a spot where gunpowder had torn it in two. Behind the headdress was a folded blanket. I moved the candle closer. It was also Native American: a perfect shawl for a shaman to use to conceal "her" face.

141

I shivered, though the closet was warm. "I've got to get out of here," I whispered.

But I couldn't. Not yet.

On the other side of the closet was a makeshift altar on a small wooden bookshelf. On the top shelf were two candle stubs on either side of a large lump covered by a black cloth. On the next shelf lay a pack of American Indian tarot cards and a familiar peace pipe. On the bottom was an old leather-bound book which looked like a diary. I reached for this.

The worn cover shook as I opened it. The first page had yellowed and warped, though the ink was still legible.

There was no date on the entry. The handwriting looked frantic, as if the person writing it was panicked or out of control.

It read: "Vince! Oh, god, Vince! Why did you have to die? You're the only friend I've ever known. Why did this happen? It was me. Oh, god, it was me. The Spirits wanted to punish me again. Oh, Vince, I'm sorry. They killed you because of me. My friend, this I vow. I will speak to them. I will find out what it takes to appease them. And then you will not have died in vain."

I shook my head and reread the passage. I turned the page.

A different handwriting, printed in the forced block letters of a grade-school child, asked: "Can I marry her? Can I? Please. You'd like her. Her name is Melanie and she's pretty. She's got the blood. You know, our blood. Caddo blood. We can have a baby so the Spirits can live. That's all they want: just a chance to live. I know, 'cause Manitu told me. I know you'll like her. I'll marry her and then you'll love me."

I couldn't believe what I was reading. It was so crazy. Melanie. Where had I heard the name? I stared at the candle trying to remember. And then I knew. I recalled that first evening when Dr. Broussard and I had sat alone on the back patio. He had mentioned a Melanie. Frankie said she'd died.

The diary drew me like a magnet. I didn't want to read on. I was afraid of what else I'd find. I turned the page.

In a different handwriting, I read, "She is tainted. The Spirits are furious with your offering, cur of the white man. You must send her to me to see if by herbs and supplications the Spirits will cure her barren womb. If not, I will send for Stalking Moon. Manitu Flying Eagle has spoken."

I slammed the book closed. My heart shook my body with each beat. "He's insane. He's truly insane. Of course all those strange events seemed crazy. They *were* crazy."

I pictured the hooded figure in the corner of a cabin in the woods. No wonder the shaman never took off her shawl. It was Dr. Broussard under there all time. Dr. Broussard, and yet not him.

I tried to remember the conversation when I had asked Manitu Flying Eagle if the enemy she kept referring to was a man. "It is the same," was her strange reply.

"Of course. Why didn't I see it? Dr. Broussard is the shaman and himself. Female and male, it's all part of him." But I didn't understand, not really. How could anyone understand it?

I ran my fingers over the cracks in the leather binding. He warned me about an enemy, and yet he wanted to help me discover that it was him. Why? But if Dr. Broussard was insane, why even ask why? "Why" assumed there was a reasonable answer. Terror began to rise in me.

I opened the little book again and flipped over a few pages. I found another entry in a similar style as before. "The spirits have rejected her womb. They demand an offering. This woman, who was born malformed, must die as the Ancestors cut out the life of their disfigured infants. Stalking Moon comes."

143

Drawn to the pages with a morbid curiosity, yet repulsed by their content, I read on. The next entry had been written by someone gripping the pen and bearing down so hard that in a few spots the page had been torn.

"Oh, great Spirit of my Ancestors, your servant has completed the task. We have sent the Wasichu to you and have tasted her body and blood. Her head we offer to you. Her heart and liver mingled with the smoke of the pyre. Her bones reside with our ancestors."

I couldn't believe it. My stomach knotted and a sour taste reached the back of my throat. When people were murdered on TV, it was so easy to not get really upset. But this woman had lived. She had had family who cared for her. And she had been murdered—by her husband—the same man now married to Frankie. With a rising panic, I flipped through more pages looking for anything which might be significant.

Many of the entries were nonsense, as "bomb, Mom, death, the spirits, the spirits, to the center, fall apart . . ."

I came across another one printed in block letters. "I'm lonely. Please come play with me. I'm sorry. I won't bother you any more. No, please, not the spirits. I'll be a good boy, you'll see. Stop. Don't hurt me. My legs are bleeding. No more, please. Hug, please, hug. Don't hurt me."

A lump grew in my throat for the little boy who had been so tortured. But had it happened to Dr. Broussard? Or had he hurt a little boy? Or was it all the insanity? I didn't like the possible answers to any of these questions.

The next script was different from those which had come before. It was organized, professional. "I'm going to marry Francine. She is a good woman. I don't want any objections. I won't stand for them. I'm in control now. You will not hurt her."

What was this? Did Dr. Broussard have his insanity under control when he met and married Frankie?

144

Many pages were blank after that. At last, I found more writing. It was in Manitu Flying Eagle's hand. "Petersen is going to dig up the bones. This must not happen. You cannot keep us away, now, Walter. We must protect the bones. Stalking Moon, you must frighten him off."

Stalking Moon responded: "Wasichu. The dirty Wasichu. He freezes as an animal which is stalked. Yet he does not turn from his task. I want his blood, not his fear."

"No. You must persist as the spirits have commanded, Stalking Moon," Manitu replied in writing.

Again, I skipped a few pages until I found Stalking Moon's writing. "Two Wasichu women violated the holy rites. I have cursed them. As they saw my power, they fled. The younger one must be watched. She is strong."

Pieces of the puzzle fit together in my brain. I remembered a figure standing on a moonlit mound, arms outstretched as if in worship. It had been Dr. Broussard, or at least the part of himself he called Stalking Moon. He chased Mother and me and clung to the car window, his hand clawing at my throat. And later he arrived saying he had been at the liquor store. Every time the "spirits" appeared Dr. Broussard wasn't around.

I scanned the closet. I spotted the deerskin outfit, undoubtedly what Stalking Moon wore. I saw that the knees of the pants were torn and dirty and wondered if they had become that way when he had clung to the car the first night I was in Weches. And as I examined the costume, I realized with some relief that at least Stalking Moon was not dominant in Dr. Broussard at the moment because the outfit was here. At least, I hoped it was true.

Half hidden by the costume, a tape recorder and loud speaker leaned against the wall. I reached for the "play" button on the recorder, then decided against it. The noise would alert anyone nearby. I knew now I would hear "Wasichu, dirty Wasichu" from the tape.

Manitu had raised the herbs, both the deadly monkshood and others which supposedly had magical properties. As I read, I saw that out of fear for Frankie's life, Walter had "gone" to Manitu for herbs that would protect his wife. He had placed these under Frankie's mattress, in her closet and at her office. Walter wrote to the others in a way that revealed his fear; he wouldn't stand for any interference with her the way they had "interfered" with Melanie. But his warnings lacked conviction.

Turning the page, my eyes were glued to it. Manitu's writing proclaimed, "Francine intends to deny the Spirits life. She uses poison to kill the egg. She is no better than Melanie. No, she is more evil. She plans to prevent the Spirits their road into this life. At least the deformed Melanie sought ways to change her fate for the better. Francine asks us to take a knife to her. Stalking Moon, the Spirits command you. They rage in anger at this sacrilege. Take her! Take her!"

There were no more entries. I slammed the book closed.

My pulse raced. Dr. Broussard intended to kill Frankie. That day Frankie and I talked about her birth control pills, he had apparently overheard us and pretended he hadn't.

"What am I going to do?" I panted as the panic reeled in my mind. "I've got to find her."

I dropped the diary on the floor. A slip of lined notebook paper fell out, and I could see that it had been torn from a spiral notebook. Carefully unfolding it, I saw that it was from my journal. It was my poem, "Rage," which described my feelings about my mother. It gave Dr. Broussard, or Manitu, all the information he would have needed to persuade me of his, or her, "magical" powers that first time at the shaman's hut. I stuffed the paper back in the diary. I felt foolish for having believed any of it.

146

I leaned forward to the candle, about to blow it out. I stopped myself. I saw the black cloth covering something on the altar.

With dread nearly freezing all movement, I haltingly reached over and slid off the cloth. A bleached white skull stared back at me with unblinking eyes. I lurched back and screamed. I knocked the candle to the floor and it went out. My hand fell on the diary, which I clutched.

I scrambled out of the small door, slamming it shut. It wouldn't close. Ties from the tie rack were caught in the opening.

I backed out of the outer closet. I bumped into something soft. I screamed again.

Whirling about, I saw Dr. Broussard's robe hanging on the half-closed closet door. I dashed out to the bedroom and slammed the door shut. I leaned against it trying to collect my thoughts.

The house was hostile. I was torn between my desire to be safe and my duty to find Frankie.

I stumbled to the hall door, stopping to listen to the rest of the house. The air conditioner came on with a creak, sending another wave of adrenalin through me.

"I've got to call Frankie." With a burst of courage, I ran to the kitchen.

Next to the beige phone on the counter was a personal telephone directory with lists of frequently called numbers written down by Frankie and Dr. Broussard. I thumbed through it quickly, but didn't find Frankie listed. I looked under E for English Department, but it was not there either.

I shook my head at myself. "Of course. Don't most people have their spouse's work number memorized? We didn't have Dad's number written down at home."

I called directory assistance. I tapped my foot impatiently waiting for someone to answer. I groped in the drawer for a piece of paper and pencil. Retrieving one of each, I jotted down the number the computerized voice gave me.

I dialed the English Department. "Is Dr. Stevens there, please? This is an emergency."

"Oh, I don't know," the flustered student replied. I could hear her calling to those around her. "Has any one seen Dr. Stevens? There's an emergency call for her. . . . No, I'm sorry, miss. No one seems to have seen her. I'll ring her office for you."

One ring, two, three, four, five, six. Hurry and pick up the line again, I mentally yelled at the receptionist. Nine, ten.

"I'm sorry, there's no answer in her office. Would you like to leave a message?"

What am I supposed to say? Don't go home because your husband is insane and wants to kill you?

"Just tell her that it's urgent that she calls Callie. It's a matter of life and death. Do you understand?"

"Yes, I understand," the student replied more seriously. "And I'll tell the department chairman. We'll try to find her from this end, ok?"

"Thanks. That would be great. We've got to hurry and find her."

"We'll do our best, miss."

I hung up, standing still for a moment. I needed some sort of protection.

I ran down the hall to my room, deciding to take the hunting knife with me. "I guess I should have turned the knife in to the police as evidence long ago. I'm glad I didn't, now. But where am I going?"

I opened the door and walked to the dresser. On the top, leaning next to my make-up mirror, was a folded note with my name on the outside. It was from Frankie. My heart sank.

"Dear Callie,

"My lovely, spontaneous husband has decided that we need to spend some time alone together. It's not that we

148

don't enjoy your company, but you know how newly-weds are.

"Anyway, on the spur of the moment, Walt called me at the office and suggested we go camping in the woods for the weekend. He has everything planned and all I have to do is get in the car. He says he wants to show me a beautiful view.

"If you are alarmed about staying by yourself, I'm sure the Petersens will be glad to have you for the weekend. We'll be back on Sunday. Be careful. Love, Frankie."

The note dropped from my hands.

"Oh, Frankie. How am I going to find you now?"

Fifteen

I picked up the phone and dialed. I had to get help.

"Sheriff's office. May I help you?"

"Roger Bailey, please. This is an emergency."

"One moment please."

"Deputy McKinney." A woman's voice answered.

"I need to speak with Roger Bailey. Is he in?"

"No, he's out of the office. Can I help you?"

I squeezed my pounding forehead. "No. Uh, yes. I mean, I need to speak to him urgently. It's a matter of life and death."

"Calm down, now. First of all, who am I talking with and where are you calling from?"

Her calmness helped to slow me down. "Callie Davis. I'm staying at Dr. Walter Broussard's house. My mind just went blank. You'll have to look up the address."

"Ok. That's fine, Callie. You said this is a matter of life and death. Can you explain? Take a deep breath first."

"I'm the student who found the bones out at the archaeology excavation. I've just found out who was in that grave. It's Melanie Broussard, former wife of Dr. Walter Broussard. I found his diary describing how he killed her. And I found her skull." I was talking faster and louder. The pitch of my voice went up. "You've got to help me. He's going to kill Frankie. We've got to stop

150

him. He's crazy. You've got to tell Sheriff Bailey."

"Take it easy, Callie. Who is Frankie and how do you know he's going to kill her?"

"Dr. Frankie Stevens, his present wife. He wrote in his diary that she had disappointed the Spirits just like his first wife because she didn't want to have any children. So the Spirits want her to die. He's crazy, like I said, and thinks he's some sort of Indian executioner. Listen, Sheriff Bailey will understand."

"I'm sure he will. In the meantime, I'll send a squad car around to pick you up. We'll need to get a statement from you and see this diary before we can arrest anyone. I take it that you haven't actually seen Dr. Broussard threaten Frankie."

The panic inside me began to turn into anger. This woman didn't understand how urgent the situation was. "No, I haven't, but you don't understand. There isn't time. I've told you, he's going to kill Frankie. They've already left town on a camping trip. He'll kill her in the woods, just like he did to Melanie."

"I understand, Callie. But I have to make sure you're safe, too. I'll see you in this office within an hour. Bring that diary."

My head hurt as I hung up the phone. I willed myself to relax, hoping it would ease the pain and clear away the frustration so I could think clearly.

"Ok, I obviously can't wait around here, whether or not it puts me in trouble with the Deputy." I glanced down on the phone table to where the old brown diary lay. I picked it up, held it slightly away from my body. "I've got to take this with me."

The thought of trying to stop a killer by myself frightened me, and I impulsively dialed Bart's number. Erica answered.

"Erica, this is Callie. Is Bart there?"

"Oh, hi, Callie. How are you? How are the clothes working out?"

"Erica, this is urgent. Is Bart there?"

"Nope. I think he's working. Why? Did you two ~~~e a fight?"

"Is your dad home?"

Her voice became concerned. "No, but he should be soon. What's going on?"

"Listen, I found a diary written by Dr. Broussard. He killed his first wife and now he's going to kill Frankie. I tried to contact the Sheriff, but he wasn't in and the Deputy wants me to come into the office. Dr. Broussard's taken Frankie out into the country and he's going to sacrifice her. The body that I dug up was Melanie Broussard. Do you understand?" My rush of words sounded like garble to me.

Her tone was very serious. "Are you sure, Callie?"

I nearly shouted into the phone, and knew I'd cry out with frustration if she didn't believe me. "Erica, I found the skull to the body in Dr. Broussard's closet with a lot of other weird things. It looked like a type of altar. And I've got the diary where he describes what he did to Melanie and what he's going to do to Frankie. I've got to stop him before he hurts her, but I had to tell somebody. We have to find her before——."

"Ok, ok," she said quickly. "I don't have a car, but Dad will be in soon. Which way are you headed?"

"I'll check the site first." I paused. A vision flashed through my head. I was in my square digging. I felt I was being watched. I looked up and spotted a tower. "Oh, god, I never thought of that. He wants to show her a view. There's a fire tower within sight of the mound. Did you ever notice it?"

"Sure. Everybody climbs it."

"I've got an eerie feeling about it. I'll go there next." She gave me directions to the tower, told me to be careful, and we hung up.

That first night in Weches, when Mother and I were lost, we drove down a dirt road and had edged up to a car parked next to a clearing. I pictured the moon rising over a mound with a figure on it. The last piece of the puzzle fell into place. The mound the man had stood on was the one I would excavate a few days later. We had interrupted Dr. Broussard as he performed some sort of ritual on Melanie's grave. I shivered down to my toes at the thought.

I walked into the kitchen, grabbed the extra set of keys to Frankie's car and my purse from the counter, and entered the garage. While the garage door opened, I got into the car and started it. Before putting the car in reverse, my eyes glanced to the fuel gauge. The tank was nearly empty.

"Great!" Looking at my purse, I remembered I was out of cash. Staring back at the fuel gauge, I thought, "I guess it's the only chance I've got," and pulled out of the driveway. I decided to leave the garage door open, hoping it would tip the police off to something being wrong.

I raced down the street, barely pausing for a stop sign. I drove as fast as I could without losing control, glancing from side to side and in the mirrors for police. In a university town, they were always on the lookout for young speeders, and I hoped one would spot me. Maybe I could talk a patrolman into going out to the site instead of taking me back to the station.

At the outskirts of the hilly city, I shook my head at the rearview mirror. "Why is it that when you really need a cop, you can't find one?"

The fuel gauge read empty now. "Is it empty when it's on E, or when it's below E? I guess I'll find out."

The four-lane highway leading to the excavation site narrowed into two, winding in and around the pine forest and over hills. As the car headed up an incline, I saw the fuel gauge drop, only to move up slightly on the downside.

I barreled down the road. It straightened for a stretch of a mile or more before it curved behind trees again. A

153

fear came over me that he was hurting Frankie right now. I pressed down the accelerator, and saw the needle drop below E.

The entrance to the excavation was only a couple of miles ahead. I made it around the next few bends and over the next hills. I checked the speedometer. I was doing 80 on curves marked 45 m.p.h. I accelerated on the down slopes hoping the momentum would carry me over the top of the next hill. The expected sputtering started as I climbed the last hill before the site turnoff.

"Come on, baby. Don't give out on me now."

My hand grabbed the gear shift, ready to shift into neutral should the engine fail. At least I could coast a little farther after that.

Right before the crest, the engine died and I popped it into neutral. I leaned forward as if this would help the car up to the top.

It slowed, but to my relief, it cleared the top. I aimed it around the bend and toward the entrance to the site down below.

The little Toyota picked up speed. Just before I began the turn onto the dirt road, I realized that perhaps I was going a bit too fast.

The road to the excavation was pretty long. If I braked, it would slow my speed too much. And the sooner I had to walk, the more time it would cost me—and Frankie.

The car entered the turn, and I willed it to hug the road. In a moment of panic, I realized I had not fastened my seat belt.

My hands gripped the wheel tighter. The tires rolled off the asphalt onto the dirt, and the car leaned as if the outer tires might come off the road.

"Don't spin out," I commanded through gritted teeth, and avoided the brakes so that the car wouldn't flip.

My senses seemed to extend to the tread on the tires. My mind gripped the road like a cat extending its claws.

A pothole approached. I barely turned the wheel, urging the car gently to one side. Any sudden change in direction could send it rolling.

I made it past the pothole, and let out my breath. Now all I had to do was avoid the rest of the holes. The car was slowing its hell-bent speed.

I aimed as close down the center of the rutted road as I could. As it slowed, I pulled the car to the edge of the clearing where the bus usually parked and stopped.

I was all alone.

I had never felt in so much danger. A feeling of panic swept over me. I wanted to stay inside the locked car. I'd hunch down out of sight until the police or Dr. Petersen came. If the madman came after me, at least I'd have a knife.

I groped for the weapon which I had shoved in my purse. I gripped its handle and shuddered.

"If you stay here like a coward, Frankie will die. And I can't imagine that Stalking Moon will make it pleasant for her. He stabbed Melanie many times."

And with that, my resolve firmed. Seeing nobody around, I opened the door. I shoved the diary in my purse and pushed it under the front seat. Locking the door, I put the knife through one of my front belt loops and the keys on top of the front tire.

With a glance toward the fire tower, I whispered under my breath. "He's not expecting you. You've got the element of surprise. And you've got to use every advantage you have."

An anger toward him arose inside me as I trotted away from the car. How dare he try to kill her! So she was taking the pill. It was her body. I knew Frankie was a sensitive person. If children were a big need in his life, I knew she would consider it.

My breathing had become deep and rhythmic as I ran. I shook my head at my attempts to understand Dr. Broussard's behavior. It was just hard to believe that the kind professor I had lived with was totally crazy. It didn't make sense. How could he seem so normal to so many people?

The fire tower above the tree line lay across the large rectangular clearing. Although I didn't feel someone watching me, I was positive that he was there.

My eye ran down the trees from the fire tower. There in the remote corner of the now pock-marked meadow was a slight break in the line of pine trees. That was where Mother and I parked that first night.

Ironically, I realized that I had just taken the long way to the site. I had gone the most direct route from the University, but there was a shorter route from Frankie's house. As a matter of fact, the site would have been rather convenient if someone had known about the old logging road.

And someone had.

I kept to the trees as I pushed through the brush near the road, now easing the knife out of the belt loop and into my right hand. Walking on the empty road, I followed clear tire tracks toward the tower.

My senses were keenly tuned: I heard the varied call of a mockingbird in a tree overhead and the quiet noise of my sneakers crunching dirt. The faint tartness of evergreens mingled with the choke of iron-rich dust. My tongue tasted dry and bitter.

Here I was—both hunter and prey. How well I kept my wits would determine which I would ultimately become. And though he had had a good chance to study me in his own home, he didn't know that I understood a few things about him.

Ahead the road dead-ended. A sense of danger urged me into the trees. I moved carefully, avoiding twigs and loose rocks in the dirt.

Dr. Broussard's car was parked there. He and Frankie stood at the base of the fire tower. Her wrists were tied, her face blanched in terror.

Sixteen

I froze. My heart thumped so hard that it shook my body slightly each time it beat.

Dr. Broussard brandished a long knife at Frankie.

Again, panic overwhelmed me. What am I going to do, run up with my little knife and yell "drop it" to him? He looked like "Stalking Moon" who attacked me, though he was dressed in khaki pants and shirt, not the buckskins. He had found a way to put the war streaks on his face, which no doubt added to Frankie's horror.

Ok, ok. I have to think about this calmly. I have to distract him. Frankie has just had the shock of her life, realizing that her husband wants to kill her, so I can't count on her to help me wrestle him down. She'll probably be torn between her love and fear of him. So I have to find a way to come between them. She might at least be able to run.

A rock. They always toss a rock as a distraction in the movies. But I'll have to shove her away, or at worst, force him to attack me. That will give her a chance.

Broussard's back was to me. I moved through the woods toward him. Thorny bracken tore at my bare arms and legs, the scratches turning into bloody welts. Each foot stepped carefully between scattered sticks and twigs. Most of the ground was covered with a layer of soft pine needles that absorbed the sound of my steps. The closer I got, the more I could hear of their conversation. He was speaking of how she defiled the Spirits, and her head was cocked to one side, her face confused and unbelieving. It was unlikely either would hear me as I approached.

When I was within ten feet or so, I paused and searched the ground. At first, I feared that I wouldn't find a rock to throw. I made myself look methodically from left to right. I saw one as large as a baseball. I had to squat down and twist awkwardly in order to reach it. I was relieved when I grasped the cool, jagged object.

I decided to aim at the trees on the other side of the dirt drive leading to the fire tower. That would lure his attention in the opposite direction for a moment.

I had never been a great softball player, but I knew I could throw a rock that far—if it didn't hit the trees on this side whose trunks left only narrow gaps through which to aim. If it hit these trees, Dr. Broussard would turn and see me immediately.

I gathered my courage, made careful aim, and let it fly. With a sharp whack, it hit a tall pine on the other side. He whirled toward the sound, his long blade at the ready.

I broke out of the trees, getting one last bracken cut on my right leg, and pointed my body between them like a missile. In a quick motion, I transferred the knife to my right hand.

Time slowed and each movement demanded maximum effort. With the brunt of my momentum, I knocked Dr. Broussard from behind, forcing him off balance and forward onto the ground.

Frankie gasped to see me. I rebounded from him to her, yanking her away. She stumbled into a run toward the dirt road, but I saw that she was too shocked to go at full speed and was looking back.

"RUN, FRANKIE!" The words seemed to dribble out of my mouth. I had to buy her a head start.

The enraged man, at once familiar and strange, pushed to a stand and brandished his weapon at me. He let out a cry that started as a low growling pitch and ended in a shriek of garbled syllables. I had stolen the hunter's prey.

With animal quickness he charged me. I stood for his approach, knees flexed, arms forward and slightly bent. I judged the speed of his attack. At the last moment, I dropped to roll at his feet, aiming the knife away from my torso.

A foot stumbled against my back and I heard him hit the dirt in a sprawl. I didn't stop to examine the damage I had done. I was no match in a fight with him and needed some higher ground as both a weapon and a refuge.

The fire tower. The metal stairs which wound inside the derrick-like structure began at about fifteen feet above the ground. Scanning the zigzag cross beams, I saw that I could scramble to the stairs fairly quickly. From the bottom stair platform, I could probably hold him off until help came. And I'd be close enough to the ground so that I could help Frankie if necessary.

All this flashed through my mind as I scrambled to my feet. The toes of my tennis shoes dug into the red dirt, my arms pumping at my side. I reached the peeling green structure and realized that I couldn't climb with my knife in hand. I glanced over my shoulder and saw Dr. Broussard—or Stalking Moon—starting another charge. I clenched the blade between my teeth and reached to the slanting cross bar above me. With quick movements, I scrambled up a level, glad that my tennis shoes firmly gripped the steel.

I reached for the next level and placed my right foot on it. I transferred my weight, pulling myself up to the level which would put me out of his reach.

I could feel his knife cut through my left ankle to the bone. Searing pain shot to my head. A wave of nausea and darkness swept over me, and for a moment I loosened my grip on the bar.

The loss of stability set off an alarm through my brain that pushed back the threatening blackness. I tightened my hold and lifted the throbbing leg beside the other one.

I reached for the next bar, and saw the stair platform above me. Grabbing higher this time, I instinctively supported most of my weight with my arms and moved the good leg to the next level. Even so, I had to use the wounded left foot for balance. A groan escaped my lips as I pulled the hurt limb up. I nearly dropped the knife out of my mouth in my agony. I grasped the platform and lifted my body onto it as a swimmer would pull herself out of a pool.

My legs dangled over the small square landing. My eyes focused on the large gash in the ankle, bright red blood pulsing steadily down the heel of the white shoe. Refocusing on movement, I saw Dr. Broussard reaching for the second rung on his ascent after me.

What had once looked like a safe, defensible place now seemed like a trap. I pulled my feet onto the platform and pushed to a stand. My left knee buckled at the white-hot pain and I awkwardly pushed to a stand.

My head leaned back, fighting the dizziness. The stairway circled around the frame until it ended under the floor of the top platform. There were the square lines of a trap door, but was it locked? Somewhere on my approach, I thought I had seen a sign: Private Property of the U.S. Forestry Service; Keep Out. Dr. Broussard grunted with effort, and I committed myself to an ascent.

Half stumbling, half crawling, I began up the steel stairs. Each step had once been painted forest green and had been cast with rough protrusions to prevent soles from slipping. Now the paint was worn in the center, the grips slippery with age and the steps sagging. I tried to use the left leg for balance, but a shot of blackening pain ruled this out completely. I ended up clinging to the smooth rail with my right hand and supporting my weight with both my left hand and right foot. I made it through two turns before Dr. Broussard stood on the small landing below.

Saliva drooled out of my mouth and down my chin as I continued to clench the knife in my teeth. I would have preferred moving it to my belt loop but I didn't want the delay.

I scrambled up another flight. *You certainly distracted him away from Frankie. Good job, Callie.*

His hard-soled shoes clinked on the stairs. I sped up. It might take a few moments to open the trap door. I need to buy time.

You've fooled him once with the rock and once when you rolled. Can you fool him again?

Rock and roll. Hey, that's pretty good!

A flood of hilarious laughter tried to overcome me. I fought against it. I stifled a wave of panic. I tried to recall the first aid I had been taught in Health Class. Am I going into shock from the wound? A quick check of other symptoms noted that I no longer noticed any pain, the foot seemed numb, and I felt cold and light-headed.

By now I was above the tree line. Hopping from step to step, I focused on the rolling forested hills which became bluer as they receded in the distance to the sky. I paused, tempted by as a deceptive urge to rest.

A beautiful sight . . . wish I knew how to paint . . . green hills merging with blue sky and large fluffy clouds . . . I'd use a big canvas . . .

I heard a noise below me and reluctantly tore my eyes from the landscape. With great effort, I twisted my head and saw a path of sticky red down the flight and the one below it. *Somebody made a mess by spilling all that paint . . . can't imagine that the Forest Service will look kindly on that.* Somewhere in my brain I noted a muted but frantic alarm, though I couldn't make sense of it.

I shivered despite the intense heat of the summer day. *The higher in altitude you go, the lower the temperature . . . didn't think it would be this cold up here.*

161

Still looking down, I saw a head come into view. The savage eyes hungered as they found me, and I responded like a frightened deer.

With a quickness that a part of my mind wondered at, I scrambled up the last flights to the top. As I crawled up the final few steps to the trap door, it occurred to me that I would need to use my hands to steady me instead of using them to open the door. So I simply kept moving, bracing my neck and back against the weight of the door on my head. With some resistance at first, and then lessening, the door opened and I crawled up the remaining steps. With a nudge of my shoulder, I threw it open with a bang and wiggled onto the observation platform.

Firm pressure stops bleeding. The words reverberated in my skull, and for a moment I wondered what it meant. My eyes fell on the torn tissue around the still heavily bleeding flap of skin and muscle. There wouldn't be time to use hand pressure. With thick fingers, I fumbled with my belt buckle, at last managing to unfasten it. I pulled it out of the loops and knotted the wide navy canvas firmly over the wound.

I noticed the wind for the first time. It was strong. The rail around the edge of the roofed tower offered no shelter.

On hands and knees, I crawled around to the trap door. I automatically protected my leg as I turned and sat on my rear. I stuck the tips of my fingers under the wooden door and hoisted it up. As I raised it higher, I pushed with my palms and it dropped to a close with a bang.

Just as soon as it closed, it opened again as if it were bouncing. I watched it curiously as it rose, until I understood what was happening. I threw my weight on it to stop him from coming through, but it was too late. A backhanded slash with his long knife was enough incentive for me to back away to the rail. But with careful aim, I kicked his right hand with my good leg. He released his grip and the knife clattered to the weathered floor and over the edge. I heard it hit the ground moments later.

In rage, he pulled himself fiercely onto the platform, letting the door slam shut. He saw me flinch as I realized my way of escape was cut off, and he laughed loudly.

"You have nowhere else to go, Wasichu."

I was transfixed by the yellowness of his brown eyes. The black and red streaks on his face were drawn like a target with his eyes at the focus.

With the boldness of cornered prey, I yelled back at him. "You may have cornered me, Stalking Moon, but Frankie got away. The Spirits won't be pleased."

Venom filled his eyes. "The Spirits will have an extra offering before they have her, and be doubly pleased." He glanced at the knife I now clutched in my hand and down at my angry wound. He smiled. "It won't take long to finish you. Stalking Moon will complete his work."

I forced a bravado I didn't feel. "Even if you do kill me, you won't kill Frankie. The police are on their way. I notified them before I left. I told them what I found in your diary. Frankie will meet them and show them the way here. You won't be able to harm her. You will fail." I clenched my knife.

He suddenly tossed his dark head back and howled to the sky. "MANITU!"

His head sagged forward. When he lifted it again, he was calm, controlled. He spoke in a contralto woman's voice. "The Spirits see all. The woman is tainted; the child-woman is blemished. Both must be given to the Spirits. Both hearts must be taken and bloods tasted, just as before."

Before I had a chance to discover my own psychological limits, his head sagged again. He lifted it carefully, looking at me fearfully from beneath his dark eyebrows. I saw his lower lip trembling. He hunched his shoulders and drew his arms into his body, leaning away as if he was frightened of me. "Don't hurt me," he whined in a tiny voice, edging away from me on the platform.

I pursed my eyebrows. What is going on? And then I remembered the child's printing in the diary. Emotions whirled about me: Anger, fear, disgust, pity. *I felt stronger when I pitied Erica.*

Dr. Broussard pulled his legs up to his chest and leaned against the rail, one fist stuck against his cheek and the fingers of the other hand twirling his hair about his ear. He whimpered quietly.

I had an impulse to reach out and comfort him. I wanted to say something consoling, but felt confused and scared.

He raised his eyes hesitantly to me, flinching occasionally. "I didn't mean to do it. I won't eat any more of your cookies, ever. Don't hurt me."

I opened my mouth to say something, but at first nothing came out. A flood of sorrow for him swept over me. "It's ok, Walter," I said softly.

A look of hope mixed with disbelief filled his face. "I love you, I love you. Will you love me, too?"

My heart ached for him. Without thinking, I leaned forward and reached out to touch him with my left hand, as if the touch could erase some of his anguish.

As I curved my back, the muscles in the back of my legs stretched. A blinding pain exploded simultaneously in my ankle and brain. Nausea and blackness threatened once again. My head began to swim. I grabbed for something to steady me, and it happened to be his knee.

In my stupor, I saw his head droop briefly, only to be jerked up with seething hate in his eyes. He fiercely grabbed my left wrist, twisting it painfully and causing me to draw closer to him. His eyes hungered for my throat.

He forced me to lean further down, increasing the agony in my ankle. I cried out and instinctively struck at him with my other fist.

164

It was only afterward that I remembered what I clutched in my right hand. A wave of shock passed over his face, followed quickly by a recognition of pain.

In horror, I pulled my bloodied knife out of his left shoulder with a jerk, releasing it as my arm recoiled. It, too, clattered to the ground below.

In a moment of weakness, he slumped to his side on the floor next to the tower's edge, a pool of red quickly growing around his wound. As if in faint, his relaxing muscles and gravity caused him to roll on his back toward the hot Texas ground below. His grip on my arm relaxed.

His eyes flicked open. He grabbed my arm again and turned toward me. With an evil smile, he continued to allow his body to roll beyond the railing.

I leaned back trying to counterbalance his weight. Still smirking, he moved his feet free of the only post which could have blocked his fall. His weight was supported in part by me and in part by his hip and right side. His left arm hung limply and the left side of his shirt was soaked in blood.

"Dr. Broussard, what are you doing? This is crazy. You'll kill both of us." I was forced to press my legs to the floor for leverage, and yet each throb of pain weakened my resolve.

He laughed weakly. "The Spirits want two, and they shall have two."

My mind raced. "Listen, you are sick, Dr. Broussard. It must feel scary and out of control. But you've built a new life for yourself. Frankie loves you. You can get help."

A fierce pride showed in his eyes. "I am Stalking Moon. I am the strongest. The professor is weak. I am in control, and I say he must die."

His hip slipped over the edge. I strained against the force, and for a moment thought we would fall. With an extreme effort, I stopped his movement, and he hung there with his chest and right arm remaining above, the rest of his body swinging freely. But his grip on me tightened.

I panted. There wasn't much time. My strength was almost drained.

"Dr. Broussard, you've got to help both of us. Stalking Moon means to kill you and all that you've worked for. For Frankie's sake, and for your own, you've got to hear me."

His expression went blank, and then with growing recognition, his mind fully registered the situation and all of its implications. Horror and panic seized him. "Oh, my God, my God. What have I done?" He closed his eyes and tears squeezed out of them. He exhaled silently, his body shaking. For a moment, I thought he was dead.

And then with a loud gasp, he cried, "MELANIE! OH, GOD, I'VE KILLED MELANIE!" He shook with sobs as he gave way to despair, and his body inched farther out.

I grabbed his arm which held me and tried to edge closer to a rail post for an anchor. I succeeded in moving him another inch away from me instead.

"Dr. Broussard, you've got to help me. Try to put your leg on the platform."

He looked at me in sorrow. "Callie, what have I done to you? How can I live with myself?"

We were slipping. I shouted at him frantically. "You need help. Frankie and I will see that you have the very best counseling, and we'll help you. But you've got to help yourself first!"

He nodded faintly and tried to pick up his leg. I could see that his other arm would be of no use. His foot groped for the edge of the platform, but didn't get close. He thrust his leg up repeatedly until he weakened, each time the limb dropping, causing his body to swing dangerously. I finally maneuvered to the post and wedged myself against it. The skin on my wrist burned as it stretched under his grip.

My eyes shifted to his face. I watched his eyes glaze and cheek muscles go limp. Before I could wonder about what was happening, his hand squeezed my wrist with inhuman strength. I could feel my bones pressing painfully against each other.

His eyelids narrowed and twitched, his nostrils flaring. An evil smile turned one corner of his lips up.

He's going to kill me!

"NO!" I released my hold on him with my other hand and he slipped down, dragging me by my wrist which he still held.

A small rumble escaped his throat, which I took for a laugh. He seemed to draw strength from my terror.

I fought to hold on to the railing, but couldn't find a firm grip.

He gurgled another laugh, and then laughed more deeply. But his laughter caused his body to shudder in pain. His eyes flashed as if in victory, but his strength gave out.

Before I knew what was happening, he slipped beyond my grip.

I squeezed my lids shut even as the laws of physics took over and I was thrown across the platform against the opposite rail. Instinctively, I reached out and grabbed it.

It struck me later as odd that I never heard him hit the ground. It was a trick that my brain was responsible for, but I was glad of it.

With my last ounce of strength as a nauseated darkness descended on me, I forced myself to the center of the platform by the trap door, and collapsed.

I awoke with an annoying itching sensation on my nose. I was cold. I told my arm to scratch my face and was surprised at its sluggish response. With stiff fingers I felt loose strands of hair around my nostrils. I awkwardly pushed them away, only to have them blow back.

My hearing returned. There seemed to be sirens and shouting voices in the distance. I wondered at the commotion. People were calling my name, which for some reason annoyed me dreadfully. I was simply too tired to be bothered.

My eyelids were stuck together. For several minutes, they occupied my whole thoughts. I examined them from the inside out, trying to find a weakness in the glue. In a moment, cracks of bright light pierced my brain. Despite the pain, I tried to focus, but gave up and shut them again.

Come on, coward, you can do better than that. With a sigh, I geared myself up for a greater effort, and this time succeeded.

The world was a swirl of light and dark. The confusing blur took me a while to understand. And then I knew that I was still on top of the fire tower.

I pushed weakly on my elbow. As the spinning slowed somewhat, I again saw the beauty of the rolling hills in East Texas, this time painted in the reds and purples of sunset. It comforted me to soak in the evening. Intuitively, I sensed pain and sorrow was connected to the ruckus below. When I left this tower, I knew I would be in pain for a long time.

I rested my cheek more comfortably in the cup of my hand and stared into the distance.

Bart. It would be nice to show this view to Bart.

I watched an eagle stretch its long wings and capture one last warm thermal in which to soar before the fall of night.

Seventeen

My head rested in Bart's arms, my eyes closed, but the rest of my senses were very much awake. We swung gently back and forth in his back porch swing while a gentle breeze fanned us. My leg, still in the brace, felt better elevated on the arm of the swing instead of down.

For some reason, the jasmine on the porch railing was in bloom again, and its sweet scent perfumed the air. But the lovely smell, his warm embrace, and the gentle rocking could not wipe out the sadness in my heart.

In three days, Mother was coming to take me back to Houston. Three days. I had talked her out of taking me home after the accident, but school would start soon. Bart would go his way, and I mine, and that would be that.

Then I knew. I had to stay. It was silly wanting something that could never be, but I wanted it anyway. My heart ached, and I burrowed my head closer to his chest.

"Hey, what's wrong?" Bart's voice rumbled through his chest.

My throat constricted as I looked into his big blue eyes. I could barely speak. "I don't want to go home. Since Dr. Broussard died, it's been hard, and painful. But—" How could I say how much he meant to me?

How could I tell him how grateful I was for his kindness, his friendship, his love? "Bart?"

Tears filled my eyes. He leaned over and kissed me. Wet drips fell from my cheeks into my ears. The kiss continued—long, passionate, tender.

When our lips parted, my nose rubbed his nose. "Bart, I want to stay in Weches with you."

He sat up straighter. A smile slowly spread across his face. "You do? Why didn't you tell me sooner?"

"I guess I just figured it out."

He pinched his eyebrows together in thought. "You could go to Weches State this fall instead of finishing your senior year."

Now I sat up. Other kids in my high school had done that, but they had applied to colleges almost a year in advance. "It's too late, isn't it?"

"Tomorrow's the deadline. Dad knows the Registrar, and I bet Frankie would help." He was excited.

My hope grew. "They have my transcript from when I applied to your dad's course, and I made an A in that. Mother could—" My own excitement screeched to a halt. "Mother. I'd have to ask her, and she'd say no."

Bart leaned over. "Would Frankie help?"

I nodded. "I'm sure she would talk to Mother if I asked. Frankie wants to sell the house, which I could help her with, and I'll bet I could live with her in an apartment." Frankie could hardly stand being in the house now. She was going to move soon, no matter what.

"So what do you have to lose? If your mother says no, then nothing's changed. But if she says yes,—"

If she said yes, I could start college. If she said yes, I could learn about people, and why they did what they did. Why did people go crazy? How could someone kill another person?

And I wanted to help Dr. Petersen get the mound skeletons ready to turn over to the Caddoes. They would bury them secretly somewhere, with a proper Caddo burial.

Dr. Petersen was disappointed at the court order, but it seemed right to me.

Instead of feeling intimidated by Mother, I suddenly knew I could convince her. All I had been through made her seem different. Now I saw her as if I were another person. All her anger and impatience toward me covered up her fear for me, fear that I wouldn't be able to make it in the world.

Well, I had confronted a darker part of the world than most other people had ever seen, and survived. My tough-talking mother had never faced anything like it. It was time for me to be a part of choosing the path for my life.

"I'm going to call now."

When Bart got my crutches for me and helped me stand, I felt tall enough to reach the sky.

SUZANNE CHANCE is an editor and writer who lives in Colorado with her son. In addition to writing, she loves hiking, backpacking, downhill and cross-country skiing, dog sledding, and just about any excuse to be outside in the mountains.